LEATHER BOUND

THE BINDINGS DUET BOOK 2

KATE ROTH

Leather Bound

Written by Kate Roth

Copyright © 2018 by Kate Roth

Cover Photo by For Your Eyes Boudoir Photography

www.foryoureyesphoto.com

Photographer: Ben Murray

Models: Jordon Blackwell, Kaitlyn Gibson

Edited by Wise Owl Editing

Additional Editing by All Good Things Editing
www.allgoodthingsediting.weebly.com

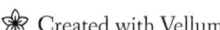 Created with Vellum

I WANT TO BE INSIDE YOUR DARKEST EVERYTHING.

-FRIDA KAHLO

CHAPTER ONE

Sloane

I told myself not to turn around. My entire walk to Black and Brew I'd kept my head down, careful not to let my eyes drift across the street. My body ached to take even a single glance at the doors, at the parking spaces out front, at the arched letters of his last name gracing the window, but I resisted somehow. I stopped outside the door to the coffee shop and took a deep breath of cold winter air. It was as if I almost felt his presence from a block away. The pull of the places that held his memory had never waned, the main reason I tried so hard to stay shut in my apartment whenever I was in Salem. This town was Leo Calloway.

My head began to turn, weakened by the thought of his name, just as the door to Black and Brew flung open. When I saw Ethan's smiling face something new fluttered inside me for a split second.

"I thought that was you," he said. "Come in, it's freezing

out here." He held the door open, his arm high on the frame so I could walk underneath and inside the building.

"Hey, thanks," I said, slipping under his bicep. The warm shop and the rich smell of coffee nearly made me moan when I entered, Ethan at my heels.

I turned toward him when the door closed and pulled at the scarf around my neck. Ethan's eyes danced across my face, a smile splitting his lips. His dark beard had grown in a little thicker since I last saw him at the Fall Festival.

"I haven't seen you in so long," he remarked. "How were your holidays?"

They'd been horrible, just like every other moment since I'd learned the truth about Leo's sister and her son. I'd kept quiet while my sister and her boyfriend and Bryon and Craig cheerily decked the halls.

"They were good," I lied. "How about yours?"

Ethan grinned and nodded, ogling me the way he had since the first time we'd met. "The holidays were nice," he replied. He edged toward the counter but never took his place behind it, as though he didn't intend to stray far from me. "So, what can I make for you?"

I glanced around the shop. I didn't spot Melanie among the handful of patrons strewn at different tables through the café. "I'm meeting someone. I might wait until they get here."

Ethan's face fell almost unnoticeably. "Leo?"

The name made me shut my eyes and blink a few seconds longer than needed just so I could picture his face. I swallowed hard and shook my head as I captured my bottom lip harshly between my teeth. I felt the pain shoot through the tender flesh and a moment of calm came soon after. The urge to do it again, a little rougher—maybe enough to break the skin—floated through me. I held back and licked at my stinging lip instead.

"No. Leo and I...we aren't together anymore."

Ethan's brow rose barely. "Oh. I'm—I'm sorry."

"Hey, Boss?"

Ethan turned at the voice with a grimace. The young woman in the black apron looked troubled as she whispered something to her superior. Ethan sighed and just as my eyes swept back to the door to see Melanie walking in, he spoke.

"Duty calls," he said with a pained smile.

Melanie waved as she approached. I swallowed thickly, knowing what I hoped we'd talk about when I asked her to meet me. I forced another smile for Ethan. "No worries, my friend just arrived. It was good to see you."

His eyes danced across my face and unease mixed with intrigue settled inside of me. "Don't be a stranger, Sloane," he said before taking off with his young employee.

Melanie's full lips split in a beaming smile and she pulled me into a hug. "You look beautiful," she whispered in my ear before letting go.

The compliment stunned me, not just because of the suggestive scratch to her quiet voice but because when she said it, I felt beautiful for the first time in weeks. I stumbled through a thank you and we made our way to the counter to order drinks before finding a seat near the fireplace.

Though we'd only met two times, conversation started

easily between us. I asked about her daughter and she shared a few stories of motherhood. She asked about my family, how I grew up, and my jobs through the years. Questions like those were part of the reason I didn't often make new friends. Half of my family was dead and my job before I came to Salem was working for the man I was having an affair with. I skimmed the details for her, steering our idle conversation away from my heavy baggage. What I'd come to ask her about was heavy enough. In the half hour we'd been talking, she hadn't asked me about Leo, but I'd been thinking of him from the moment we sat down, my question for her brimming on my lips. I assumed she knew we weren't together anymore but didn't know how much of the story she'd heard from him.

My coffee was nearly gone when silence fell over us for a moment. It was that perfectly-timed lull in chatter that afflicted every conversation. It was borderline awkward as Melanie caught my gaze and narrowed her eyes. "Talking with you has been wonderful, Sloane, but I'm wondering... what did you really ask me here for?"

I gulped, attempting to swallow my urge to chicken out and keep our conversation light.

One corner of her mouth tilted up and she took a sip of her tea. "In your message, you said you wanted to ask me some questions and I didn't imagine your questions would simply be about my life. Is there something you want to ask me?"

My mind flashed a memory of my palm cracking three

times against Leo's cheek and the urge to move forward with my life won. "Do...do you think I could be a Domme?"

Melanie scanned me, her eyes lit with surprise. "Do you want to be a Domme?"

I tongued my bottom lip then brought my thumbnail to my mouth, catching it between my teeth. "I don't know," I whispered.

Melanie sighed and placed her hand gently on my knee. "Is this about Leo? He told me you two broke up."

"You saw him?" I despised how quickly I bit the line she threw out.

"No. I called him to invite the two of you to our home for another get together and he told me."

"So...he...he didn't go to your party?"

Her pained smile made me hate myself. I hadn't spoken about him at length in months and I told myself that meant I cared less and less each day. But that was bullshit. Every day my heart ached deeper. Every flash of a tall, dark-haired man made my stomach sink. And each mention or thought of his name made my insides tremble with regret and longing.

"No. I haven't seen him. He didn't come to the party."

"How did you know you were a Domme and not a sub? People can be both, right?" I asked, steering the conversation back.

She nodded absently as she mulled over my question. "I'm very passive in my day-to-day life. Many of my previous jobs were based around serving others. Before I met my husband, I was a doormat. I know I'm a Domme because it's the role I choose to play. Taking ultimate control is a thrill I only know during sex, but Dominant is who I am deep within. I can't explain it, it just is. But, you're right, lots of people consider themselves Switches. I... well, I don't know you well enough to make an assumption as to what role you're better suited, but..."

"You think I'm a sub."

Her tight-lipped smile was answer enough. "If you're serious about trying it, Gabe and I know some subs looking. We could arrange an introduction."

I crumbled. "No. I—I don't think I want that. It's just been on my mind. I shouldn't have even brought it up."

"There's nothing wrong with trying different things. How else do we learn what we enjoy?" Melanie met my eyes and leaned in closer. "I think you know what you enjoy, Sloane. I think you know who you are already but maybe the problem is that you no longer have a counterpart."

A painful pulse of anxiety worked its way from my kneecaps to my hips and settled in between my shoulder blades. I knew saying something nasty wouldn't make her statement any less true. I doubted she knew how deeply those words cut me.

"We know other Doms too...our home is a safe space if you'd ever consider being paired with someone else."

Bile tickled the back of my throat and this time I couldn't keep the outrage from painting my expression when I glared at her.

Melanie registered my opposition to her suggestion and threw her hands up in surrender. "Or not," she chirped.

"Sloane, honey..." her voice softened and my bristled state slowly diminished. "Before you even think about getting involved with someone else—Dom or sub—you should talk to Leo. He's just as torn up as you are—"

I sucked in a sharp breath, cutting her off. "I'm sorry, Mel," I said, glancing at my phone. "I have to run. Thank you for meeting with me. I'm glad we got to chat and get to know each other. We should do this again. Forget I said anything about the other stuff. I've just got a lot on my mind, you know?"

I rose and Melanie followed, her mouth twitching open and shut as though she wanted to beg me to stay, or to talk to Leo, or consider meeting one of her other kinky pals to play with, but I cut her off again and pulled her into a quick hug.

"This was nice. I needed to get out of the house. I'll call you." She sighed again and said goodbye, though her face said a million things more.

I tried to keep my head clear of damning thoughts as I rushed out the front door, tossing my cup in a trash can on the way. The biting air stole my breath for a moment as I bundled back up, buttoning my coat and securing my scarf around my neck. I trudged along the slushy sidewalk, every step a little faster than the one before. I kept my head down and soon it all played out in my mind just as it always did— every perfect moment with Leo leading right up to the worst one. When I realized the common denominator between us and the lie he'd held onto. Leo had kept from me the devastating truth that his sister had been Warren's mistress long before I was. That I wasn't special. That what

Warren and I had—no matter how fucked up in its own right—wasn't new or unique to him at all. I left Warren when he got his wife pregnant, something he promised he never wanted even with me. But it turned out he already a child—a child who was Leo's nephew. While Warren was first getting me into bed, Leo's sister Marie was having his son, Barry, now an adorable, curly-haired four and a half-year-old. It was an intricate spiderweb of lies and deceit and every single thread of it made me feel like the dumbest woman on the planet. *Red. Black!* My brain screamed safe words at the thoughts as though they'd stop their assault, but the memories and the vicious part of my mind that aired them behind my eyes didn't play by rules.

"Sloane!"

I instinctively turned my head at the sound of my name but regretted it the instant I realized the direction my eyes pointed. Across the snowy street, I saw Wendy waving at me from in front of Calloway Books. She smiled but I couldn't react. I stood paralyzed as I gazed past her at the store I'd once loved so dearly. Wendy hustled across the road, pulling her long sweater jacket tightly around her as she bobbed in front of me.

"Hey, girl," she huffed.

"Hi."

Wendy eyed me as her breath hung in the air as fog. "We all thought you moved."

My eyes flicked to the door of the bookshop again. *We.* Was he inside? Was he watching us? "Nope. I'm still here."

"So...um...I know with everything that happened you

won't be at the store anymore but...Oliver and I, well, we're getting married..."

"Wow."

She smiled and nodded before lowering her eyes, her hands sweeping over her abdomen lovingly. "I know, right? All kinds of surprises, actually."

I should've never left my apartment. Wendy was a nice girl. Probably the kind of girl I could've really found myself getting close to through our mutual love of Calloway men. But that wasn't my path anymore. As sweet as she was and as happy as I was for her and Oliver, I didn't need one more Calloway child popping into my mind reminding me of what I'd never have.

"Anyway, I don't want to be huge and swollen when I'm a bride, but it's important to Ollie that we get married before the baby's born so it's happening in a few weeks." Her hand jutted out, pushing one square, cream envelope and another long envelope with a clear window on the front into mine. "You're invited. I know that's awkward and I won't be upset if you don't come, but Ollie and I miss you around the store and Leo, he's absolutely—"

"Wendy, please," I croaked.

I couldn't take one more mention of him. I couldn't take one more splinter of him digging into my heart. I didn't want to hear how sad Leo was without me or how much he missed me. He did that to himself.

Her face fell and she reached out to touch my shoulder. "I'm sorry. Anyway, your last paycheck is there, too. Just think about it, okay?"

I forced a smile and nodded, feeling the wind on my cheeks as they warmed with irrational anger. "I'm happy for you. Tell Oliver that."

Wendy squeezed my arm and turned to hurry back through the front door of the shop as I stood stunned by the sight of eyes peering at me from the across the street. A cloud of smoke flowed from his mouth, over his face, and into the sky as we stared at one another. My eyes burned the same moment my mouth moved into a smile.

With that, I turned and pounded my feet into the sidewalk, not looking back at Leo, berating myself for the betrayal of my curving lips. I tried not to smell the air in hopes of a whiff of clove smoke, but when a hint of the scent entered my nose—possibly imagined—my mind offered a worse treason with a single thought. How lovely it was to be near his mouth again, even in the most indirect way.

CHAPTER TWO

Leo

Between the bitter cold wind, my increased smoking habit, and the look she'd just given me, my chest throbbed painfully. I thought her smile would give me some sense of hope. But, no, Sloane didn't smile at me the way she used to. It was the kind of smile you offered a stranger when they made eye contact with you in line at the bank or passing in the produce aisle. The quick flash of Sloane's teeth and the curve of her ruby lips hurt more than if she'd flipped me the bird and spit in my direction. That forced, distant glance startled and wounded me more than the weight of her hand slapping my cheek all those nights ago when it ended.

I pushed through the front door and marched straight to Wendy. "What did you say to her?"

Her face screwed up in an offended grimace. "Nothing. Jeez. And let's just get this out of the way now; I'm not playing middle man for you. If Sloane reaches out to me,

I'm not passing her love notes or anything. I won't jeopardize my friendship with her for whatever BS you did to make her run away."

Fucking Wendy. My brother's choice for a bride hadn't ever seemed like a problem until Sloane left me and the questions set in. She attempted to interrogate me after I walked in to Oliver's house alone the night of the family dinner, but I never told her. I never told anyone besides Ben. Even Oliver tried to dig into it, but I knew it'd get back to Wendy, my parents, and God forbid, my sister Marie. As badly as I wanted Sloane back, the thought that constantly troubled me was a reasonable one. How could she reenter my life and be a part of my family knowing what she knew? How could she ever look at my nephew again without the pain of knowing she'd been sleeping with the man who abandoned him while he was an innocent little baby? And how could she forgive me for keeping that secret from her?

I let out a heavy breath and dragged a hand down my jaw. I'd given up shaving for the simple fact that I wanted to look in a mirror as little as possible.

"Wendy, I just want to know if she said anything about me."

She raised her arms, tying her hair up in a bun on top of her head, a superior half-smile plastered on her face as she glared at me from behind the register. "When I said your name she cut me off. She sure as hell didn't bring you up. She doesn't even want to hear your name."

I nodded absently, swallowing the knot of emotion that

shot up my throat. "You invited her to the wedding though?" I asked quietly.

Wendy softened, maybe after seeing what a kicked dog I became after her snappy retort. "Yeah. I gave her an invitation. She may not come, though," Wendy said. "Don't bank on it, Leo. Maybe you should just let her go."

I'd tried. I'd tried to forget what it was like to be bound to someone. I'd tried to rid my mind of the memories of having a perfect match. I'd tried, damnit. Letting go seemed impossible.

A strong hand clapped my shoulder and I turned to see my brother's face. Though I hadn't shared with him the circumstances of the end of my relationship with Sloane, he'd been a solid support. Oliver had always been the strong, silent type and it turned out that was exactly what I needed.

"You all right?" Oliver asked.

I nodded my usual silent thanks before heading to the office. I'd taken over more of the clerical work so I could stay closed in that little room away from all the places that reminded me of her. Oliver knew I wouldn't go up to the second floor anymore where our entanglement began. Thankfully, he was happy to let me be the man behind the computer for once.

Closing the door behind me, I pulled out my phone and tried her number like I did every day. Maybe since she'd looked at me just minutes ago, she'd weaken and pick up. When the robot voice recited her number in my ear, I hung up. Her voicemail box used to begin with a message from her. I'd call every day just to hear her speak. But the day after I left a message admitting that fact, the robot answered instead, depriving me of another piece of her. I had no one to blame but myself.

———

"One more round," Ben pleaded. "I'll pay for the car home."

My head had clouded by the third round. I didn't truly think I needed a fourth, but it had become just as much of a habit as smoking. Drink her away. It was nearly laughable. I'd turned into the masochist—happily filling myself with poison day in and day out. Waking up every morning to a headache and a cough reminded me I was alive. It reminded me I deserved to feel like shit.

If Ben hadn't been a foot taller than I was and outweighed me by eighty pounds, he would've been in just as rough shape as I was the mornings after our nights out. He never complained of a hangover. He took shots like they were water and chased them with beer, barely finding himself tipsy at the end of the evening.

He signaled our waitress and a few blurry seconds later, she arrived with two more drinks. I swallowed the burning liquor just as Ben spoke.

"We've been here for a few hours and you haven't mentioned her."

"And?" I said with a scoff.

"So, what, she's off your mind suddenly now or something?"

I glared at him over the top of my glass as I poured half of it down my throat.

"Leo, you look like shit. All you do is work and drink."

"All *you* do is work and drink!" I snapped.

Ben laughed. "True, but I look great."

"I saw her today."

Ben's eyes grew wide. "Did you talk?"

Staring down into the shallow pool of bourbon remaining in my glass, I shook my head. "She looked at me and pretty much sprinted in the opposite direction. She hates me. It's time for me to give up."

I knocked back the rest of my drink and met Ben's stare. His gaze narrowed on me and my words settled like a heavy boulder in my stomach. Defeat lingered and though I hated the feeling, I knew it was right. I didn't know how I'd ever get her to respond to me, let alone take me back.

"Okay," Ben said, slapping his palm on the table. "I'll talk to Jade. I think she knows a few subs looking around. We'll set you up."

The rock in my gut grew tenfold and threatened to shatter my ribs, pressing insistently against my heart. A quick flash of images made the liquor in my belly pitch. Me with someone else. The idea of placing black gloves on the flesh of any woman besides Sloane repulsed me. I sucked in a sharp breath through my nose. If I gave up Sloane, I gave up being a Dom.

With alcohol and anger flooding my mind, I thought of the pathway that led me to the lifestyle in the first place. As a teenager, I constantly found myself in trouble. I hated authority—my parents, teachers, the law—it didn't matter. I refused to take direction because I was positive I knew better. But at the same time, I lacked confidence in everything I did. By the time I was eighteen, I was angry and disillusioned and figured college was the opportunity to reinvent myself. I wanted to get out of Salem and figure out who the hell I was.

Diana Casey was the sole reason I stayed in instead of going to the college parties that most likely would've landed me with an arrest record. Despite finding a girlfriend, there'd been no remedy to my lack of confidence. I was a complete coward around Diana. She made every move and I was the consummate deer in the headlights. One night, she asked me to take the lead and I told her I didn't know how.

She said to fake it, to pretend. Role play.

It was amazing how easily that came to me, putting on a façade, playing that I was strong and cool and desirable. Pretty soon that confidence didn't only come out when we were fooling around and after a while I wasn't pretending anymore. I'd uncovered a part of me that I'd never understood and as I discovered more and more of that dormant self-assurance, I flourished. I stood taller and acted with purpose. It was clear that Diana was growing more attracted to me and who I was becoming. The first time I held her arms down and pinned her hips with mine as we kissed, it all came to a head. She begged me, and it was as if a light switch went on inside me. I went from a kid who wrestled with his identity to a boy playing at a man's game to a man who knew exactly what he wanted and how to get it.

Looking back, I'm lucky I never truly harmed her. I scared myself with her in the beginning, when I learned just how rough I liked to play. Over time, I came to understand that I had a very specific idea of the right kind of partner and, as her interest plateaued, it became clear Diana wasn't the one for me.

My chest constricted as I remembered drawing on Sloane's skin with crimson lipstick. I marked her as mine. She was the one for me. The only one. Coming back to Salem after spending years away, the last thing I'd expected was Sloane Montgomery and her easily-claimed flesh claiming my long-forgotten heart.

"No set ups," I said firmly.

Ben's mouth turned down as he seemed to realize his mistake, but he nodded. "Okay, man."

CHAPTER THREE

Sloane

"I love my husband, but I'm about ready to kill him. First, he makes me put off having this party for *seven weeks* because of work and then he forgets the cake! Sloane, honey, are you sure you don't mind?" Craig's frantic voice asked through the phone.

"I'm positive," I assured him, closing my car door and slinging my purse over my shoulder. "I'm already here. I'll grab the cake and be at your place in fifteen minutes. Take a deep breath."

I never knew such drama could accompany a one-year-old's birthday party. Bryon had forgotten to pick up the cake before the shop closed the previous night and Craig was nearing meltdown status because of it. While the two of them decorated, cooked, cleaned, and fought, I offered to pick up the cake and a last-minute bag of ice before guests started arriving.

"Thanks, sweetie. They opened at nine, so Reagan should be there. I'll see you soon."

I hung up and headed across the parking lot to Reagan's Bakery, admiring the pink-and-white-striped awning and adorable cupcake logo. The new sweet shop was just around the corner from my old office and as if I needed any more reasons to be glad I no longer worked for Warren, my waistline was surely thankful to not be tempted by the idea of afternoon treats. I pushed through the front door and heard a bell ring, a sound that turned my stomach almost instinctually. Shaking away the thought, I glanced around at the empty bakery and slowly made my way up to the counter. My eyes swept over the glass case full of dough-nuts, cookies, and cupcakes, my mouth watering. I looked up again when I heard a noise coming from beyond the swinging doors behind the counter. I figured I'd give it a few more minutes before I rang the courtesy bell near the regis-ter. It was early and they were probably just getting started for the day. Folding my arms, I perused the rest of the small shop while I waited. I turned at the sound of a giggle followed by the swoosh of the swinging door to the kitchen and nearly dropped a tin of enticing gourmet popcorn.

A young brunette wearing a pale pink apron stood on her toes near the edge of the glass case, kissing a set of lips that I could still remember the taste of. My stomach lurched, my heart constricting painfully. His deep, sultry laugh when she bounced down to where she stood a foot shorter than him made my skin crawl. She turned to me with a bashful look then smiled.

"Hi there, can I help you?"

I stared blankly at her before turning my eyes to Warren for the first time in nearly a year. His mouth lifted in a smirk as he stepped toward me, curiosity lighting his gaze. "Sloane?"

My throat ached as I swallowed back the slew of curse words I wanted to spit at him. I needed to grab the cake and run but he kept me paralyzed while his newest conquest stood watching our exchange.

"Warren."

His smile turned saccharine and he cocked his head to one side. "When did you come back to town?"

Scanning his soft brown waves and chocolatey eyes, I thought of Barry and wanted to cry. I glanced over his shoulder to the cute baker and shifted my jaw, realizing how young she looked. A girl that young with her own business? A hateful wonder chased through my mind. Maybe she didn't need her rent paid for, but this storefront lease had to cost a pretty penny.

"I..." I paused and steadied my breathing. No. I wasn't going to explain myself to him. He didn't need to know any of my business—where I lived or otherwise. I shook my head and took a few steps past him toward the counter, forcing a smile.

"I'm picking up a cake for Bryon Hartley," I said. "It could be under Craig."

Her mouth fell open for an instant and her eyes flicked to Warren before she nodded. "Yeah, I'll go grab it," she said, pushing through the kitchen doors.

A hand came down on my shoulder and I shut my eyes, shrugging out from under the weight of his touch as I turned. "Don't."

His brow knit together but his smug grin never faltered. "Come on, babe. You take off one day, quit behind my back, don't answer my calls, and don't speak to me for months? Can I at least have an explanation?"

"What good would that do? Looks like you've moved on just fine without me."

He grimaced and lifted his chin toward the back of the bakery. "Reagan? She's a nice girl, but she's not you. I've missed you. Would you just talk to me? We could get coffee."

A startling dark laugh fell from my lips and a little relief waved through me knowing my gut reactions toward him had changed. "I only have one thing to say to you," I sneered. "Congratulations."

His lips pursed and his brow furrowed fiercely. "How many times do I have to apologize? I thought Elaina was on the pill. But...honestly, since we've had Chloe, I've changed my mind about a lot of things. If you'd just talk to me—give me another chance...I'd be willing to consider it now."

I clamped my teeth down on the inside of my cheek so hard I feared I'd taste blood. A heavy breath stretched my lungs and I pushed down the sickening feeling he filled me with. In one step, I closed the distance between us and shoved my fingertip into his expensive suit. "Let me get this straight. I haven't seen you or heard from you in close to a year, I've just caught you with another woman, and you want to *talk*? Because since you've had a child with your wife, you've *changed*? How? You're still cheating. Are you seriously saying you want me back and you'll give me a baby—even though you already have a child with your *wife*—while your *other mistress* is in the next room? What is wrong with you? Do you hear the things that come out of your mouth? Do you know how disgusted you make me?"

Warren frowned and took a step back from me, pushing my hand from his chest. "When did you turn into such a bitch?"

"When I found out about your son," I spat.

"I have a daughter."

I heard the kitchen doors swing open and leaned in close to him, a scowl on my lips. "Oh, I know," I hissed. "I'm talking about your other child. The one who didn't seem to change a goddamn thing about you. Barrett Calloway."

Before he could respond, I turned to admire the pink cake box on the counter. "They paid when they ordered it, right?" I asked as cheerfully as I could.

The young brunette nodded, a little squeak coming from her lips. I grabbed the box and breezed past Warren without a glance and marched toward my car. The chilly air stung my eyes, tears threatening to emerge. All I could focus on was the walk to my car, to freedom. I slid the box onto my front passenger seat and buckled it in for safe measure. When I walked around to my door, I heard my name. Warren's voice sent ice water down my spine. I swallowed hard and reached for the door handle, the sound of his thudding feet echoing in my head. I flinched when his hand covered mine.

"Sloane, stop!"

"Why?" I snarled, shaking him off. "Why should I stop? Why should I let you talk to me after what you did to me?"

His eyes zeroed in on my face but I turned away, not willing to let his charm cast a spell on me yet again. "What did I do, Sloane? You knew the situation."

"Does she know the situation? Does that poor young girl in there know? Does she know that you're married? That you'll never leave your wife? That you're fucking God knows how many other women? That you have at least one child you don't claim? Should I go tell her?"

His hand gripped my bicep so roughly I cried out and pulled far enough away from him to back myself against my own car door.

"What the hell is wrong with you?" he growled.

My chin trembled and my stomach raged with acid. "It was bad enough when I knew I came second in your world, but to know I was truly third...maybe even fourth or fifth...it makes me hate myself more than I hate you."

"How did you find out about Barry?"

My brows jumped. I reached for the door handle again. "That's all you have to say?"

"Sloane!"

I shoved Warren back with a strength I didn't know I had in me and climbed in my car, locking the door. He stood on the other side of the window, expression furious, hands balled into fists. With the steel and glass between us, I sighed relief. I shut my eyes and took one heavy inhale before I set my gaze on him a final time.

"Fuck you, Warren," I said as I peeled out of the parking lot.

———

I'd been hiding out in the kitchen with my bottomless glass of wine for the last few hours of the party. The birthday girl had been in bed for a while but Bryon and Craig's friends and family had lingered, drinking and celebrating. I made myself useful, cleaning up the dishes and boxing up some of the remaining food.

Bryon walked in with a smile on his face and took the platter I was currently drying from my hands. "Who knew a baby's birthday party could turn into such a rager, huh?"

I chuckled and gestured to the countertop lined with empty wine bottles. "No kidding. Just imagine her sweet sixteen."

He finished drying the platter and placed it in a cabinet before facing me, leaning back against the island. "You've been hiding in here. Is everything okay?"

"Yeah, yeah. I'm fine. I just don't know a whole lot of people and you know me, I tend to wallflower at these kinds of things."

"I'm sorry," Bryon whispered. "I know it must be hard. I can't tell you how much we appreciate how much of a presence you've become in Elizabeth's life."

I'd taken to the role of aunt rather easily, but Elizabeth

was an easy child to love. Looking at her didn't help ease the pain of missing Leo, missing Barry, missing my chance yet again. Rebuilding my relationship with Bryon, forming a bond with Craig, and connecting with Elizabeth had brought a little more meaning to my life in the past few weeks. But after seeing Warren, it'd all been dragged to the surface again. Our end, his betrayal, Leo and everything that followed. It was pain upon pain and I felt as though I couldn't breathe.

Bryon reached out and put a hand on my shoulder, snapping me out of my thoughts. "Sloane? What's wrong?"

"I saw Warren today," I breathed.

Bryon stiffened and I felt the immediate anger radiating off of him at the mention of Warren's name. "Where?"

Choking on a laugh, I scrubbed my hands over my face. "He's fucking the bakery owner."

"Jesus!" he exclaimed throwing his hands in the air. "Reagan? How the fuck does he do it? What kind of superpower does this asshole have that turns smart girls into complete morons?!"

I pinched my bottom lip between my teeth and felt tears sting my eyes. He wasn't wrong. In fact, it was a great question. One I'd often asked myself.

Bryon sighed and shook his head. "Fuck, I'm sorry. I didn't mean that."

"You did," I replied softly. "It's okay. With Warren and now Leo, I'm starting to think I was never a smart girl to begin with. I keep choosing the wrong guy."

Silence hung in the air and I took the moment to gulp what wine remained in my glass.

"Leo wasn't the wrong guy."

My eyes snapped up to meet his and while his brow rose, he didn't back down despite my clear anger at his assertion.

"He made a mistake, Sloane. He should've told you the truth, but one mistake shouldn't erase everything that was good about him. You and I made mistakes with each other but in the end, we loved each other enough to move on."

"That's not the same thing at all," I retorted. "He took advantage of me. He knew something I didn't and he used it against me. And worst of all, I let him hurt me."

"That's what you're really mad about," Bryon muttered, turning to sweep crumbs off the counter absently.

I grabbed his arm and made him look at me. "What's that supposed to mean?"

A heavy sigh fell from his lips and he narrowed his eyes. Bryon had always been one to tell the truth; he didn't know how to sugarcoat. It was part of the reason I loved him as a friend, but it was also the reason we'd drifted apart before.

"You don't see it. I know the truth about his sister and her son and Warren hurts you. It's awful, truly, and the way it all went down was fucked up and damn near Shakespearean, but that's Warren's mistake. Warren is the one you should blame for that. You act like Leo did this to you, but he didn't. You want to know who you're actually angry at? Yourself. You're mad at yourself for being vulnerable again. If seeing you this way didn't make me so sad it would almost be laughable..." He shook his head then took me by the shoulders to meet my eyes meaningfully. "Sloane, you're punishing yourself for letting go for once, for admitting and acting on the things that turn you on, for enjoying it, for falling in love with him...for falling in love with submission."

I sucked in a sharp breath. Bryon knew almost every aspect of my relationship with Leo, right down to the sex. In the beginning, I'd been so shocked by the things I felt and the things I wanted. I had to tell someone, so I confided in my best friend. Now I wished I'd never shared any of those intimate details.

Pulling away from him, I sniffed and poured myself another glass of wine. I swirled the rich burgundy liquid and glared at him. He was absolutely right. He and I both knew it and as he reached to pour himself a glass, watching me gulp down alcohol with tears in my eyes, I knew he regretted saying it out loud.

CHAPTER FOUR

Sloane

I shut my eyes and cursed my feet for leading me there. I'd been thinking about it for days, and it was as if I was on autopilot. Bryon had gotten in my head and as soon as I made it back to Salem, I began obsessing about seeing Leo again. Maybe I should at least talk to him, let him explain. Maybe I should give him another chance. Every time I considered it, I felt stupid. I remembered the sinking feeling in my stomach when I first understood the depth of the secret Leo had kept from me and I talked myself out of going. As my mind went back and forth, caught between the intrinsic draw I felt toward Leo and the whisper in my mind that told me I was sick for still wanting him, I somehow ended up in my coat. I unconsciously bundled myself up and by the time I was present again, I was standing across the street from Calloway Books, the spinning arrow of my soul set on giving him a chance.

And then I remembered asking him if he would've ever told me about Warren being Barry's father had I not found out on my own. The look on his face told me he would've kept that secret indefinitely. I remembered all the ways he used to confuse me, dominating me in the bedroom with such unyielding power then taking me for a picnic under the stars and asking permission to kiss me. It was just like I'd told him in the end—everything he did felt calculated.

I stared at the doors of the bookstore and gulped down the knot in my throat. I pushed forward, not spending another moment staring at the lights on inside wondering if he was working, not letting him control my actions anymore. I popped into Black and Brew and figured I'd grab a hot drink and head home, calling it a moment of weakness or a quick stroll for some fresh air.

Inside, I looked around and yanked open the buttons of my coat. I stared up at the chalkboard drink menu and offered a quick smile to the man behind the counter. "Is, um, Ethan working?" I asked.

"Yeah, he's working the bar," he replied, hooking his thumb to the side.

I'd never ventured to the bar tucked in the back of the coffee shop behind the huge wall and fireplace but with a quick smile, I headed there in hopes of seeing a familiar face. The moment I saw Ethan standing behind the bar, I paused. We barely knew each other, just acquaintances or new friends at the most. But every time he looked at me he lit up. I'd known since the day I met him, when I showed up in his coffee shop, offering cross promotion ideas with Leo's bookstore, that he was hoping I'd be more than a friend one day. He turned and caught my eyes as a wide grin spread across his lips.

"Sloane!"

My legs stuttered and I lost the ability to move for a split second before taking the last steps toward him. Maybe today was that day. He leaned his inked forearms on the bar top, smirking at me with glittering eyes.

"Did you come to drink or keep me company?"

I pulled in a breath. The spinning arrow in my head, the wheel of destiny, the compass I refused to read accurately found a new target. One that made my stomach less sick and the tension in my chest lessen. I took a seat at the bar and slipped out of my coat.

"Both," I said with a smile.

I stuck my tongue out and mocked a gagging noise, pushing the tasting glass back toward Ethan as he chuckled.

"Okay, not a fan of the stout," he said, swiping the empty glass before filling me another pint of the Scottish ale.

I waved him off, shaking my head. "You're getting ready to close. I should get out of your hair."

His brows dipped in the center and a smile sat in the middle of his scruffy beard. "Don't make me drink alone. Once I lock the front door I'm going to have to catch up with you."

A giggle passed my lips and I cringed internally. I watched as Ethan walked his two employees around the dividing wall toward the front door. He was gone a few more minutes, counting out the cash drawers and putting money in the safe for the night before shutting off the lights to the coffee shop front half of the store. When he appeared again, he eyed me while pouring himself a beer then claimed the barstool beside me. He lifted his glass and I returned the gesture, tapping my beer to his, my eyes secured on his lips. Shit. I already had that tingly face feeling. My lips would loosen any minute if he said the right things. And though I knew everything about it was wrong, I craved his touch merely because I wanted a man's hands on me.

He asked me about myself and I gave him the short version like I had with Melanie before directing the conversation to him. By his second beer, he was the one with the loose lips, telling me about the band he used to be in and growing up in Oklahoma. Before long, the beer was flowing and we were singing nineties sitcom theme songs behind bellows of laughter. I didn't know if it was the beer, if Ethan was easy to talk to, or if I just needed a night of fun, but I felt lighter and happier than I had in the nearly three months since Leo and I broke up. A night where the conversation didn't inevitably turn to Leo was refreshing. As helpful as Bryon had been through my break up, every day seemed to hold a sliver of a therapy session.

Ethan sighed and gulped the rest of his beer before reaching over to fill his glass from the tap again.

"We're racking up quite the bill," I commented.

He made a noise and took my glass to top it off. "On the house. These kegs are about to skunk anyway."

I laughed. "I see how it is. Make me think I'm special when really you're just clearing out your inventory before it spoils."

His sexy grin paralyzed me. "You're special, Sloane. Trust me."

I sighed and let my eyes close briefly. "Don't look at me like that," I whispered.

"Like what?"

I met his gaze and felt my senses cloud. The irrational desire to reach out and touch his beard flickered through me and made my stomach tremble. As though he saw the wheels turning in my mind, a little snicker crept out of him as he slid a hand through his messy brown hair. I couldn't answer so I just shook my head and let my tipsy mouth split into a shy smile.

"So, uh, you're not working at the bookstore anymore?"

So much for our conversation not making its way back to Leo.

"Nope," I said into my glass.

"I've heard they have quite the selection over there," he said with a little chuckle.

I shot him a look and shrugged, confused by his remark. He laughed heartily. The beer must've been getting to him too. An apologetic expression washed over him as he shook his head and quieted his laughter.

"Sorry, I'm not laughing at you. The other day one of

the baristas, Fallon, came in here absolutely losing his shit because I guess his girlfriend took him in there and showed him this entire section of like, bondage books. I didn't know there were books like that and I really didn't think you could get them at a little book shop in Salem. Guess there's some kinky shit going on in this town."

I pressed my lips together, smothering my smile. For once, the mention of the store and the memory of that section didn't hurt me. I let my eyes flip to Ethan as I lifted my beer, a smirk still lingering. As I put the glass to my lips, I spoke.

"Don't knock it 'til you try it."

Ethan gaped at me, then grinned, turning on his barstool to face me fully. "Oh really? Tell me more, Mistress."

My breath caught and I put down my glass. *Mistress?* The title sent a ripple of excitement up my spine. Maybe I had it in me after all. Maybe I just needed a new counterpart to try new things with.

I choked out a little laugh and shook my head, too nervous to say anything about the subject, not knowing how serious he was. But when Ethan's hand reached out to settle on my thigh, I shivered and sighed.

"I know I'm supposed to tell you I'm sorry you two broke up...but I'm not," Ethan said softly. "You're so beautiful, Sloane. I think about you all the time."

I glanced down at his hand and swallowed thickly. That hand was an offer and not a demand. It was bare and gentle and the opposite of Leo. And while I didn't hate how it felt, it reminded me of the touch I missed. Sucking in a breath, I impulsively darted forward and pressed my lips against his. His beard was the second difference I registered. It didn't scratch me the way I imagined it would and my fingertips rose to stroke his face as I allowed the kiss to deepen.

Ethan tasted like the beer we'd been drinking and the quiet moan he released into my mouth struck a flame inside me I wasn't expecting. My hand moved to grip the back of his neck and take control, clutching his hair, moving him how I wanted. Without breaking the connection of our lips, I moved off the barstool and snaked in between his thighs. His arms encircled my waist and I felt fingertips brushing under my shirt. Ethan's hands were rougher than Leo's, the pads of his fingers callused from years of playing guitar. My mind wouldn't quit comparing the two of them as he coaxed the hem of my top up, his touch a question.

I pulled back, pressing my mouth into a line as I panted through my nose, looking into Ethan's astonished eyes. They were the color of rich chocolate, not the icy blue I craved. He scanned my face, pupils dilated, irises bouncing across my features. "God," he whispered. "I can't believe—"

"Shut up."

The tone of my voice surprised me. An apology nearly slipped out until I saw Ethan's brows jump and a little smirk pull at his mouth.

"T-take off your shirt."

A slow grin curved Ethan's lips as he tugged the black t-shirt over his head and tossed it to the floor. I let myself gaze at his chest and once again found myself tallying the differences between Ethan and Leo. The bright colors of the tattoos covering Ethan's arms, chest, and abs dazzled me but also made me long for the firm, bare chest I loved. The rough smattering of hair across his pecs drew my attention and I touched it lightly. He looked different, felt different, smelled different, tasted different. I supposed I was different now too. The bit of confidence that began to simmer in me after giving just two commands felt different...though I didn't know if it felt good yet. My heart and my core ached simultaneously as I accepted what I'd chosen to do. I lifted my shirt and cast it to the floor, reveling in the sound he made when he saw my near-naked torso.

"Touch me."

Ethan's hands rose to skim up my sides and glide over the satin cups of my bra. I let go of a breath and held his gaze while I unbuttoned my jeans. The first time I'd had sex with Leo, I wasn't thinking about Warren. I'd lost all concept of what his touch was like—how different he was— the moment Leo claimed my body. But as Ethan pulled down the straps of my bra, lowering the cups to give his mouth access to my nipples, I couldn't help but think of Leo. I shut my eyes and let my head fall back, enjoying the touch of another man while picturing the one I wanted in front of me. Ethan's breath on my skin was a cloud of Leo's clove cigarette air. His fingers toying with my breasts were the rough touches of black leather gloves. And as Ethan's face met the crook of my neck, his whisper of, "I want you," was an intoxicating echo of "good girl."

Guilt waved through me, knowing I was using Ethan to

move through my pain. His hands swept over my skin and as I melted against his fingers, I swallowed the mounting emotion that threatened to destroy me. What was I doing? My mind hummed with a racket of doubt. I hated how much I still craved Leo.

Giving in to Ethan's caress, the room blurred as we rushed through our movements. Shedding clothes and switching places, he hoisted me onto the stool, dipping me back to lean against the bar. His mouth roamed my skin, bringing forth breathy sighs as he dropped to his knees to taste me between my legs. My hands held his face against me, threading through his hair, enjoying the kind of freedom Leo never allowed. The feeling of his dark beard against my thighs as he sucked on my clit flashed more truth behind my eyes. He wasn't Leo. I opened my eyes and picked a spot on the ceiling where I could focus as he eagerly worked to please me.

It felt good. It felt better than good. And I wanted to feel good after all this time. But I couldn't let go to the moment and surrender to Ethan. I couldn't get Leo out of my head. The ghost of him stood behind me, gripping one hand at the nape of my neck and the other around my throat. I heard his voice in my mind. *Your pleasure is mine. I'll give it and I'll take it away.*

Ethan's mouth moved to my thigh and kissed its way up to my navel where he peered up at me, lust clouding his vision. When I met his eyes, I shook away Leo's psychological grasp and yanked Ethan toward me, slipping my palm greedily around his cock. He moaned and rocked forward, catching himself with firm hands against the bar. My skin buzzed with a craving for pain but I swatted that away too, biting my own lip hard to quell the desire.

I guided him toward my sex and heard him gulp. "Hang on," he panted and slipped from my grasp. He dropped to the floor and dug in the pocket of his jeans before letting out an exasperated groan. He rushed out of the room but returned before I had time to call out his name. When his face came back into view, he leaned in and kissed me. The gentle kiss split me in two. Tenderness radiated from him as he pulled back and winked at me, showing me the condom he'd retrieved. When my face fell, his brows dipped together in concern. He brushed the apple of my cheek with his knuckles.

"Is this okay?"

Yellow to slow. Red to stop. Black to end. I wanted those options. I wanted my colors and my limits laid out for me. I wanted him to read me the way Leo did. I wanted my eyes to speak volumes that only he could hear so I wouldn't have to use my words. I wanted to be bound and gagged and bent and taken, but the utmost tenderness in Ethan's eyes told me he'd never be that kind of lover. He was caring and wonderful and I was lucky to have his thoughtful question hanging in the air. The phantom of Leo returned over my shoulder and whispered in my ear. *Do you want to fuck Ethan?*

"Yes," I croaked. "Fuck me."

His lips parted and his eyes grew wide for a split second before he put on the protection with hasty hands, holding onto my hips as he plunged inside me. I arched my back and Ethan groaned, thrusting with a gentle rhythm. For a moment, I lost myself to the feeling of him and his strange and new body. He fit me well and every time he retreated, I felt tingles swim through my veins as his touch slowly drifted me toward ecstasy. I felt his hands grasp my ankles and secure them around his waist as he moved in and out of me. His palms pressed into my hips, pulling me to him so he could settle deeper inside of me each time. With my eyes closed, I saw Leo watching me with a shaming stare. Licking my lips, I realized the idea of him seeing this betrayal made me want to act wilder. I wanted my actions to hurt him. My hands reached for my breasts, gripping them and plucking on my own nipples as my hips bucked hungrily against Ethan. I envisioned Leo's hate-filled stare and his promises of punishment.

"Deeper," I begged.

Ethan's breath huffed out and his fingers dug into my waist as he slammed into me.

"Harder!" Words spilled out of me uncontrollably.

My spine knocked against the edge of the bar and my eyes flew open to see the determination on Ethan's face as he fucked me roughly. I reached out to him, sliding my hands through his hair and down his shoulders, where I braced myself for the pounding. He clenched his jaw and pinned me with his gaze just as he lost control, grunting as he came. My core pulsated but never clamped down on Ethan's cock in a full orgasm. As I breathed in deeply through my nose, I cursed Leo for being right. My pleasure was his.

"Fuck," Ethan breathed as he loosened his grip on my body. He pulled me toward him, embracing me, and I tried not to stiffen. A ripple of self-hatred rebounded through me when I realized what I'd just done.

"That was amazing," he whispered.

I pushed him away slowly, burying the sudden emotion that swelled inside. "Yeah," I said. "I should get home though."

Dejection painted him before he nodded and handed me my clothes, shrugging into his, trying to meet my eyes.

As I zipped my jeans, I forced a smile. "You were great. I had a good time tonight."

He smirked and dragged a hand through his hair, swiping the sweat that peppered his forehead over the chestnut strands. "Can I, uh, get your number?"

"Sure." I took his phone and entered my digits with trembling fingers, then handed it back to him. The way he gazed at me, just a few inches taller than I was, basking in an afterglow I didn't have the opportunity to share, frightened me.

His smile softened and he bent to kiss me one last time. "I'll walk you to your car, just let me finish closing up."

"No, I'll be fine," I blurted, knowing I'd walked there and not wanting his company on my way home. "I'll talk to you soon."

I watched his mouth twist, fighting the urge to say something. Eventually he nodded and winked, sending another pang of regret through my heart. I slipped on my coat and headed out to the street. Under the glow of the streetlights, I saw the way my hands shook. As the wind picked up, I caught the scent of him on my skin and felt sick. My feet hurried toward home but I couldn't stop myself from turning my head at the right moment to look at Calloway Books. My heart stammered in my chest when I saw the lights still on inside. I halted on the sidewalk and held my breath when I saw him walk by the front window.

Without thinking, I glanced in either direction down Main Street and since no cars were in sight, I toed through the snow toward the bookstore. My skin still warm and sticky from sex, I could think of nothing that I wanted more than a reprimanding for my actions. I didn't have it in me to give Leo another chance yet, but I needed that sweet release only his gloved touch could offer. I didn't know how I'd get it, but with a clouded mind and a weakened heart, I had to at least try.

CHAPTER FIVE

Leo

I hustled to the front of the shop when I heard the bell above the door ring out.

"Sorry, I should've locked that. We're actually closed..." My words disintegrated on the air the moment she came into view. The burgundy hair framing her ivory face stopped me in my tracks as forcefully as a brick wall. I wanted to rush to her but something held me down. The look in her eyes as I searched her face, still stunned by the vision of her so near to me, was familiar but I couldn't place it.

"You're here," I breathed.

I watched her throat work and her eyes shift around the store. The force holding my feet down lessened and I took a few steps toward her. My chest burned the closer I got to her. My lungs ached desperately, knowing I was breathing the same air as her for the first time in three months. My hand floated up, intending to reach out to her, but the face she made as she eyed it told me to withdraw.

"Can we talk?" I asked. "I—I've been calling you."

Her eyes fell to the floor as her lips parted and her shoulders hitched up.

"Are you going to say anything?"

Sloane's head shook indiscernibly, making my brows tense together.

"Then...why did you come here?"

Her head snapped up and she quickly tucked her hair back behind her ear with a shaking hand. My heart thrummed angrily as I saw her open her mouth to speak, no sound emerging. Finally, her exasperated sigh and the glossy look in her eyes struck me and I remembered how to read her. My gaze narrowed and I stomped forward, closing the gap between us. Rage and despair swarmed me watching the way she seemed to relax a little when my footsteps fell heavy and my chest broadened.

I took her chin between my fingers and forced her face upward so I could glare down at her. The tiny breath crossed with a moan she sucked in at my touch broke my heart.

"Speak," I growled through clenched teeth.

Sloane's ruby lips puffed out a pant and she shivered under my fingers. "I—I shouldn't be here," she said, slipping from my grasp, turning her head and covering her face with her hands.

"You're goddamn right you shouldn't be here."

She spun and gaped at me. "You don't get to speak to me that way," she spat. "Not after what you did."

"I've tried to apologize. I've been trying to talk to you," I said, stepping into her space once more, turning myself into a wall before her. "I'm sorry for lying to you. But if you won't let me explain...Sloane. Clearly I upset you, but I don't know how to fix that if you won't talk to me."

Her chin rose and she turned away from me though she didn't inch back from my body.

I reached for her and delicately traced her jaw. "But I think I can tell...you're here because you want me to make you forgive me."

I watched as she scraped her teeth across her bottom lip after her little pink tongue made it glisten. The palpable sexual energy that leached out of her at my suggestion hardly moved me. I'd decided mere hours ago to set her free and move on. While I loved her and wanted her back in my life, in my arms...in my restraints, I wouldn't do what she was trying to get me to do.

"Not going to happen," I whispered.

Her face contorted and she pulled away from me once more, pushing toward the front door. "Good. I don't need you to *make me* do anything, Leo. And I don't have plans to forgive you."

"Then why are you here?" I asked again, pressing my words out.

She gulped, her lower jaw jutting out as she traced her angry eyes over me. "To say goodbye."

"Liar."

Her brows shot up and I regretted calling her that instantly.

"You have the nerve to call *me* a liar?"

I threw my hands in the air, breathing out steam as we both moved toward each other with fire in our eyes.

"Yes, you're a liar. You're not here to say goodbye or to yell at me. Sloane, do you think I don't see what you're doing? I know that look and I can see you glancing toward the stairs like you want me to take you up there. You came here to be scolded—I just wish I knew what for. I know how badly I hurt you, but just because I fucked up—just because you make me weak—well, you can't top me from the bottom, Sloane."

"Maybe that's what I want," Sloane whispered.

I froze. "What do you mean?"

"What if I want to top? Not from the bottom. What if I want to—"

A dark laugh cracked from the back of my throat unexpectedly. "Domme? Domme me?"

Her eyes fell to the floor and her expression hardened. I didn't mean to laugh, but how could she think she was capable of being a Domme when her first reaction to my challenge of that fact was to lower her gaze to the ground?

"You're serious?" I balked before adding quietly, "I may be in love with you but that doesn't make me your sub."

She hit me with the most defiant stare I'd ever received. It nearly caused me to step back, though my feet wouldn't allow me to seem even the slightest bit submissive. Not with my acidic words still burning on my tongue. I loosened barely and tried to salvage the moment. "Okay, but... Sloane...that doesn't mean we can't talk about everything that happened. About Barry. About us."

"No. That's exactly what it means. I know what I want now. And it means we aren't compatible anymore," she sputtered, turning for the door.

I reached for her but she flung the door open, slipping through my fingers as tears rimmed her eyes and tension built in my throat.

"Goodbye, Leo."

"Sloane!" I called out. A foolish attempt to stop her.

The door swung closed behind her and my heart felt strangled in my chest. Suddenly the loss of control struck me and I realized the power she wielded over me even unknowingly. She owned me more than I'd ever owned her.

A pounding headache woke me from my restless sleep and I looked at the clock. The two days since I'd seen her had passed in a blur—an alcohol-induced blur—and turned my mornings and nights upside down. The green glow of my alarm clock mocked me. One o'clock in the morning. I sat up and sighed, reaching for my phone.

Ben: *Call me and let me know you're alive. I doubt you remember me pouring your ass into bed.*

I shook my head. Ben was the only person who ever sent me text messages and he knew I rarely responded to them. I scrolled down and saw a second message from him and felt my stomach twist.

Ben: *I'm done letting you drink like that in front of me. It's too much. You need to slow down.*

Dragging my hand over my face, I breathed a sigh and knew I owed him. He'd been a better friend to me in the last few months than I'd been to him in all the years I'd known him. I considered sending a reply but figured that would only worry him more. My fingers drifted over the screen and I saw the only other text I had saved staring back at me painfully.

Sloane: *I want to go to your party.*

It was from months ago, but I'd never deleted it. Back when I had no idea that I'd fall in love with her and just a few days before the pinprick of doubt about her connection to Warren first entered my mind. My blood began to boil, only causing my head to pound more as the pressure built, thinking about that asshole Warren. As I stood and moved to the kitchen for a glass of water to hopefully begin to cure my headache, I flashed back to a phone call I received from my sister years ago.

"Leo." Marie's voice instantly stole my attention away from the computer screen at the bookstore where I'd been ordering inventory. I heard the threat of tears wrapped around my name and stood up to shut the door, shielding me from the sound of customers.

"What's wrong?"

She sniffled and my stomach plummeted. "I..."

Her breaking voice shot fear through me. When I'd visited her a few months before I found out she was having an affair with a married man. The fight we'd had the night she stumbled into her apartment, tipsy and crying after what I thought was just a normal date, was explosive. I didn't expect the knowledge to upset me the way it did. I screamed at her like I was our father, scolding her for reaching out to the burning stove. I balled my fists and demanded an explanation as though I was this man's wife, wanting answers for her betrayal. I never thought my sweet sister would be so stupid and cruel.

I waited, holding my breath, and prayed selfishly that she would tell me they'd finally broken up. I wondered if their demise would be due to her wising up or if he'd gotten bored with her. Or maybe his wife would find out and force things to end. Another sob croaked out of her and I knew what she was about to tell me wasn't as simple as that.

"Please don't tell Mom and Dad," she whispered.

I exhaled deeply and tried as calmly as I could to reassure her. "I won't," I said through gritted teeth. "Just tell me what's going on. Are you safe?"

"I'm pregnant."

With that, her tears flowed and there was no consoling her. She begged me not to tell Oliver or our parents and I agreed. Over the next few days, I talked to her often and listened to her weigh her options. I kept my opinions to myself and simply gave her my support. After she decided she'd keep the baby, I told her she needed to tell our parents.

She needed a plan. As the baby of the family Marie had never really grown up; she let other people do things for her with ease and no sense of burden. Once I figured out that Warren was not only toying with her emotions, but also paying her bills, I knew getting her away from him would prove difficult.

Turns out, I didn't need to work to separate them. The prick did it for me. The second he learned about the baby, he freaked. He did the truly disgusting thing first and informed her he would finance her quick abortion and all would be well. Marie had already made her choice and despite every hint I slipped about how he might not be thrilled by the news, she still told him with the foolish expectation that this would be her ticket to a real relationship with him.

I watched it play out just as I thought it would. He offered to pay for an abortion. She told him that wouldn't happen. He told her he didn't want any part of the baby's life and that they were through, but he'd still pay to keep her quiet. She broke down. Hard.

I knew she needed me. We weren't particularly close growing up, but she counted on me in a different way than she did Oliver. Oliver was Mr. Dependable, but he was also quick to judge. I used to think I didn't care what she did so long as she was safe. I assume that's why she called me when she was in trouble.

It took me a while to figure out how I'd make it work and Oliver was pissed to say the least when I told him I planned to move to Blacksburg when she had the baby. But

I did it. I found a job there, moved in, and helped her through the biggest thing of both of our lives.

I laughed about it sometimes. I found myself imagining —praying, even—that raising a child someday with a woman I was in love with would be easier than raising one with my sibling. I thought we fought like crazy when we were children, but the arguments that came from raising Barry were hellish. Most days, the fights weren't even about Barry...they were about his father.

She'd sneak off and see him, unable to let go even after all he put her through while I sat at home with the baby. I hated seeing her throw her happiness away for him. She loved Barry, but some days it felt like he came second to Warren. I just wanted her to grow up. I wanted her to wake from his trance and take back her life. She was strong, I knew it, and if she could only get away from him, she could see it, too. Air stuck in my lungs when I remembered the words I'd spoken to her once.

"You don't need him. Take control of your life, Marie. Take control and don't let anyone else have it, especially not some man who doesn't even make you happy. He doesn't deserve it."

Exhaling a staggered breath, I felt my words wind around my heart like a snake trapping its prey before it struck the first blow. I looked down at the old message from Sloane once more and tapped out a response as the parallels between her and my sister became all the more clear.

CHAPTER SIX

Sloane

My heart raced as I unraveled the silk tie from around his wrists, releasing him from the wooden posts of his bed. Ethan smiled up at me and I looked away, focusing on removing his restraints. It was light—vanilla, as Leo would call it—but it was exhilarating nonetheless, and Ethan's panting breaths were proof of his enjoyment. But as I freed him and rolled onto my back, pulling him on top of me, I cursed myself for what I was doing.

I sighed as soon as I felt the weight of Ethan over me. Though every other minute, my mind pointed out another difference between him and Leo—their scent, their breath, the sound of their sighs—I found a part of myself that wanted Ethan for him and not just those differences. But when I'd tied him to the bed and teased him it only created jealousy within me that the roles weren't reversed.

He slowly inched toward my entrance, hesitant, as if

waiting for my next novice command. "You're so gorgeous," Ethan mused, letting his eyes sweep over my face. "I want to take your picture."

My brows rose and one side of my mouth curved. I glanced at our phones sitting on the little table he used as a nightstand. Devilish ideas swam around just before a doubt jumped in, wrecking the waters I attempted to tread. I thought maybe I could drown out my damning thoughts by now. Maybe I could dampen the flicker of Leo's smoldering voice still whispering in my ear. *You can't top from the bottom, Sloane.*

Like hell I couldn't.

Though my stomach trembled as I looked up at Ethan, I raised my arms above my head and smiled. "Do it."

He paused a beat then grinned, reaching for his phone.

My hand darted out and I caught his wrist. "Ah, ah," I scolded. "My phone."

A little chuckle escaped and he nodded knowingly, moving his fingers toward the teal and silver case covering my phone. My arms resumed position above my head, resting gently on the pillows as Ethan swiped at the screen then pointed the lens at me. I saw his beard twitch as he smirked from behind the phone and I did my best sultry gaze. With my arms up, leaving my breasts protruding and vulnerable to his touch and him on top of me, holding me down whether he knew it or not, I felt a sudden wave of excitement I hadn't felt since I'd shown up at his door. This was what I liked—what I needed.

Ethan lowered the phone and pinned me with a soft gaze. "Someday you should let me use my Nikon," he said.

My jaw tightened. He was too nice. He liked me too much. In the three times we'd hooked up, he'd yet to satisfy me, but I liked the way he looked at me. I liked the way he eagerly waited for my latent dominance to emerge and my words to turn into commands. I knew I wasn't doing it well. I barely thought I was doing it right, but he seemed all for it.

I shook my head and swallowed hard. "Take one of you," I whispered.

This time, his brow shot up and a Cheshire grin crept onto his lips. He made a face and snapped his own photo begrudgingly.

"Lower," I said.

He looked at me and let his outstretched arms move down a few inches to take a shot of his inked chest and biceps, before staring me down firmly.

"*Lower.*"

Keeping our eyes locked, he pointed the camera at his erection settled against me and I heard the shutter click. Wordlessly, I reached for the phone and put it on the table once more, grabbing the condom that lay beside it. Sheathing him quickly, I guided him inside me, reveling in the quiet groan he released against my cheek as he fell over my body.

"Ah, fuck, baby."

A shiver moved up my spine and I dug my nails into his back. "Don't call me that."

Ethan kissed my neck and I felt him smile as he apologized against it, "I'm sorry, Mistress."

Swallowing hard, I shut my eyes and tried to feel him above everything else. Above the conflict in my mind. Above Leo's ghostly presence still addling my soul. Above the scent of patchouli wafting toward me with his every thrust. I tried to focus on the way his cock filled me. The way his muscles felt under my hands. The heat he built within me as he ground his hips against mine. I wanted to slip away and spin into oblivion, but I couldn't escape the reality of what I was doing.

I was with a man I didn't love. Desperately trying to convince myself I was someone I wasn't. Hopelessly hopeful that I could wash away the imprint of the man who owned my heart, mind, body, and soul. Denying every screaming part of me that wanted to remind me that pain— what I craved physically and what I'd endured emotionally —was inescapable.

"Put your hand around my throat."

Ethan pulled back and pushed his sandy strands of hair from his eyes. "What?"

I gazed up at him and licked my lips. "Choke me."

His hand nervously trailed through his hair again then slid down his beard. "I—um...are you sure?"

I reached around and pushed his firm ass, causing him to plunge deeper into me. "Yes. Do it."

His tentative hand came forward and I held my breath for a split second as my skin lit with excited chills. When his palm made contact with my neck, his thumb pressing against my pulse and his forefinger dusting my jaw, I shuddered and closed my eyes. He held me gently and continued to move in and out of me. With my eyes shut and that slight pressure against my throat, I gave into visions of Leo. Ethan's speed increased the moment a genuine moan fell from my parted lips.

Behind the darkness of my eyelids, I saw Leo's blue stare paralyzing me while a possessive, black-gloved hand gripped my neck with force.

"Tighter," I croaked.

I reeled back in time to the moments Leo and I shared before the secret between us tore everything apart. When I surrendered to Leo completely and felt free for the first time in my life. When his heavy hand released me from the years of angst-built barriers within me.

Ethan continued to thrust, but he didn't tighten his grip like I'd ordered. I heard his breath growing erratic and his thrusts intensified, fucking me hard like that first night at Black and Brew. I kept my eyes slammed shut and tried to will myself into the spinning sensation, using the slight pressure he offered as my only guide. His grip let up as I heard him curse and felt him bury deep within me as he came.

I sighed. My eyes opened to see him pull back from my neck, running both hands down his bearded face with a huff.

"I'm sorry," he panted. He traced his fingers over the place he'd barely held onto with care. "I didn't want to hurt you. That's not really my thing. Are you okay?"

I gulped and touched his gentle fingers—too gentle to be what I needed. "I'm good. Don't worry."

He smiled and moved to lie next to me, exhaling another long and heavy breath. "You should stay the night," he murmured.

Sucking a quick breath in through my nose, I glanced over only to see him shutting his eyes peacefully. I watched as his breathing slowed and his eyelids began to twitch, his expression relaxing completely as he drifted off to sleep. He was a good guy and my gut churned thinking about how easily I'd used him. Staring at the ceiling, I tried to take enough deep breaths to lull myself to sleep beside him, but I couldn't.

I waited a few minutes, glancing over at Ethan's sleeping form just once more before I tiptoed across his room to slip back into my clothes. I snuck out the front door and headed for my car. After turning the key, I blew hot breath against my cupped hands while the car warmed up. The feeling of my phone vibrating against my thigh startled me. I reached for it quickly, noting the time on the dash before I opened the text and a split second of worry for my sister or Bryon filled me.

Leo: *I think I understand now. If it means your happiness, I'll let you go.*

My throat tightened painfully but an inexplicable smile bloomed on my lips just as quickly. I didn't read the message again. I simply stared at his name on the screen and sighed. The words I'd said to him in the bookstore while Ethan's sweat dried on my skin were regrettable. I remembered the look in his eyes when he saw me—as though I was a mirage. He looked tired. Dark circles pulled his eyes down and a short, scruffy beard the same sable as his hair covered his jaw. I'd thought of that new beard the next time I met with Ethan and hated that it made fucking him a little better—picturing Leo all the while.

Shivers had rolled up my spine when he'd gripped my chin and barked at me to speak. Lingering traces of love and devotion whipped through my veins at the sound of his voice. Then that darkness in my mind, the place still clinging to his lie, forced words out of me that I didn't mean. I didn't want to say goodbye. I didn't want to walk away. We could never be incompatible. We were made for each other. I just didn't know how to reconcile that truth with where we stood now. I wanted to know what had made him understand. And I had to find a way to show him I didn't want to be let go.

Sloane: *I thought you didn't text.*

I threw my phone in my purse, buckled my seatbelt and headed home, trying to keep my breathing steady as I waited for the sound of a reply. When I parked my car outside my building, I dug for the phone and saw he hadn't responded yet. My guts began to twist as I made my way inside, slipping off my coat and moving to the kitchen and the opened bottle of wine on my counter top. I poured myself a glass and sat my phone down beside the cork. I stared at the screen, sipping the merlot. I froze the moment his name flickered on the glass again.

Leo: *I suppose I'll do just about anything for you.*

I fumbled to pick up my phone and as I let go of a breath, I let honesty move through my fingers as I replied.

Sloane: *I'm sorry.*

Leo: *Stop.*

Suddenly, the phone rang and his name lit up. I declined the call with one forceful tap of my finger and dropped my elbows to the counter, cradling my head, feeling the dull ache of internal war plaguing me again. I gulped down a little more wine and typed another message.

Sloane: *Don't call. I don't know what hearing your voice will do. I'm sorry for stopping into the store the other night. I shouldn't have come there.*

Leo: *You don't have to be sorry. I was wrong to laugh. I can see why you'd think you should try being a Domme. I get it now. I only wanted you to know that I'm sorry.*

My brows cinched together as I stared at his words. I knew he was sorry. I knew deep down, despite my anger and the feelings of betrayal, that he'd never done anything to hurt me. He was protecting me by not telling me about Warren's deceit. Just like a safe word laid out ahead of time or the soft fur lining of a leather cuff around my wrists, he was softening the inevitable pain. Another text pinged and my heart seized in my chest.

Leo: *And I love you.*

Guilt flooded me as I caught the scent of Ethan on my clothes. The last time I saw Leo flashed before my eyes. My stomach knotted as I remembered turning my back on him and the desperate sound of his voice as he called out my name. I turned my back on a man who loved me, walking away from the only thing to make me happy for as long as I could remember.

Sloane: *Meet me tomorrow night? To talk?*

CHAPTER SEVEN

Sloane

I couldn't stop fidgeting as I sat at the table for two, waiting for him to walk in. We'd never been to this restaurant together, making it completely neutral territory for this new kind of meeting Leo and I were about to share. I'd spent the afternoon agonizing over what to wear and going back and forth in my mind about if I should even go. But when he sent me a text at five o'clock telling me he was off work and looking forward to seeing me, I felt familiar butterflies swarm.

A throat cleared behind me and I stood, recognizing the feeling of his eyes on me though I couldn't see him. When I turned, I let my gaze drift up his body. I drank in the sight of him, dressed in a gray sweater and black pants, the firm, broad chest I remembered filling his clothes flawlessly as he drew in a deep breath. The dark scruff along his jaw looked trimmed and tamer than it had the last time

I'd seen him. And his blue eyes, the ones that'd swallowed me up the first time I looked into them, looked bright. Hopeful.

"Hello," he said.

I swallowed hard and instinctually trained my gaze to the floor at the sound of his voice. He cleared his throat again and I heard tension somewhere behind the noise. Cursing myself for letting his presence alone will me into the submission I'd been craving—however subtle—I offered a soft smile and moved to take my seat.

"Hey."

Leo sat opposite me and hesitantly reached for one of the menus on the table. "Hope you weren't waiting long," he said without looking up.

"Not at all," I murmured.

The hairs on the back of my neck prickled with every word of forced conversation. Silence hung in the air for a moment and when the waiter arrived to take our drink orders, I almost felt compelled to ask him to stay to buffer the awkwardness at our table.

"I'll just have water," Leo said.

I shot him a look and blurted, "No beer?"

I watched his expression flicker from something that looked like he might scold me for questioning him to something much softer.

"I'm trying to cut back," he said quietly. "Just water."

The swift resolve with which he erased his dominance from the space between us shocked me. He offered a tight-lipped half-smile and glanced down at the menu again. I ordered water as well, sighing heavily when the waiter left us in our tension bubble once more.

"You look different," I said. When his eyes rose to meet mine, the smile on his face, surrounded by the dark scruff, pierced my heavy heart and I wondered if I'd make it through an entire meal with him.

"You look just as beautiful as the first time I saw you."

Nope. Not going to make it.

I pulled my lips into my mouth and pinched them with my teeth, tossing a hand through my hair. "So...um..."

Leo watched me closely, waiting for me to go on, waiting for my move—my direction. He was letting me lead though I could see it pained him. I almost smiled at the way he attempted to breathe deeply, to loosen his jaw after it clicked, to ease the worry lines on his forehead. As I struggled to take control, he struggled to relinquish it.

"How have you been?" I asked.

He forced out a heavy breath followed by a sad smile. He didn't answer, only shook his head. Swallowing hard, I nodded. Even without words, I understood. And I knew the feeling well. Maybe if I went first...

"I've been splitting my time between here and Blacksburg. I've been taking care of Elizabeth for Bryon and Craig some days. But I'll probably start staying here more as soon as I find a job."

"Your position at the bookstore is yours if you'd like it."

Having dinner with him took enough effort—how would I survive a day trapped with him in the place where I'd become his? And with him as my superior, no less? The thought of knowing our secret sin room remained one floor up while we tried to sort out whatever it was we were going to be now seemed dangerous. Arousing, but extremely dangerous.

"I don't think that's a good idea," I whispered.

"Right." He gave the same soft smile he'd been wearing since he walked in. I'd seen him smile before, but this one was different. It was an endless apology.

Leo's hand reached across the table, wrapping around mine without warning. The feeling of his skin on mine, soft and warm, reminded me of better days. He gazed at our linked fingers.

"I am sorry, Sloane," he said. "When I first heard you say Warren's name, I tried to tell myself it couldn't be the same man. I wanted nothing more than to erase that conversation from between us but—"

"Stop, Leo."

His head snapped up and caught my eyes. He pulled his hand away from mine so slowly it ached. "Just tell me what you want from me, Sloane. Let me fix this. Please."

"I want...to start over," I admitted with a sigh. "I want to try to forgive you and I want to remember why I trusted you. I want to be your friend. I *need* to be your equal."

He scraped his teeth over his bottom lip. "I'm not sure I can...how do we—" he stopped himself and pulled in a breath. His hand jutted toward me again, this time as a firm extension, an introduction, and he held me with the same unyielding gaze.

"Leo Calloway," he said. "I believe you know my brother, Oliver."

Two hours later I remembered why I'd fallen for him in the first place. The genuine curiosity with which he asked me about myself had always unsettled me slightly. It was like I couldn't believe he really cared enough to know. I struggled to find my words at first when he asked what I'd been doing the last three months. I left out Ethan, of course, and running into Warren. I shocked myself by letting my walls down and opening up about how I'd struggled with the quick change in my life. I told him how hard the holidays had been without him and he agreed, rippling guilt through me.

Then my levees fully broke. The sudden honesty about the dark hole that swallowed me after I left him overflowed; words poured out of me so quickly that my ears burned and my chest pulsed with anxiety. But when I finally met his eyes he nodded and I wished I could take it back.

"I understand," he started. "I spiraled. Drinking too much, not sleeping, not shaving." He laughed as he stroked the closely trimmed facial hair.

My lips tipped up in a small smile, admiring the change while hating the reason for it.

Leo lowered his eyes to the cleared table and shook his head. "I'm sorry. I don't mean to make it about me. I deserved what I got. You didn't."

"Don't do that," I said, reaching for his hand, surprising us both. "I have to own my part, too. I shouldn't have just left the way I did. I've never been that great at facing things head on. I came here running away from the last heartache; I shouldn't have done it again."

Leo stared at our hands and turned my palm upward, caressing it familiarly. My mind screamed for me to pull away, to maintain control and ownership of my body, but his touch still lit a flame inside me. His fingertip trailed down the crease across the center of my palm before I mustered the strength to pull away.

"Friends don't touch each other that way," I murmured.

"I don't want to be your friend, Sloane."

I pinned him with a stare. My jaw clicked when my teeth lined up firmly. "You don't have a choice."

I expected him to huff, roll his eyes, or grumble a snide retort, but his brows rose and a quick, small smile flashed on his face. A breath of a laugh escaped him as he looked me over with an amused expression.

"What?" I barked.

"Nothing. I'm just surprised. It looks pretty good on you. Authority," Leo said. "It looks...natural."

Squaring my shoulders, I cocked one brow proudly and reached for the check as soon as the waiter swooped past to set it down. A little noise left Leo at first but when I didn't react, he simply chuckled again.

"Very interesting," he mused.

I slipped my credit card in the leather booklet and glanced across at him again, rolling my eyes. "Whatever."

"May I ask you something? Something that a friend might not ask another friend?" he probed.

"I guess."

With a heavy sigh, he frowned. "Are you planning to find a sub?"

I shook my head quickly, avoiding his eyes. "That's none of your business, Leo."

"You're right. I just—if you do, please talk to someone like Melanie about it. There are crazy people out there. She can help you find someone to trust. It's just as important for a Domme to trust her sub as it is for a sub to trust a Domme."

I gawked at him. "Seriously? A few nights ago, you laughed in my face when I mentioned it and now you're giving me advice? You expect me to believe that you're in favor of my Switch status? You gonna offer to share your toys with me? Teach me some of your favorite methods?"

I watched his expression harden at my disdainful incredulity. The indigo eyes I'd seen light return to over the last few hours darkened, and his jaw tightened. "Is it so wrong for me to care about your safety?"

Scoffing, I turned away and stared blankly at the crowd that had accumulated in the restaurant. A part of me savored his deep concern but I fumed at the way his words made me feel like I was being a defiant teen.

"You may force me to be only your friend, but I'll continue to care about you as the woman I love," he said. "No matter what."

"I think for the time being, we should keep that topic off limits," I said, not acknowledging his last comment.

"Sure. You're obviously in control here. But what exactly are we trying to achieve by being friends?"

"I don't know," I admitted. "Just give me time, Leo. Let me lead."

He gave a whisper of a smile and acquiesced with a nod. I took a deep breath and signed the check before I stood. Leo followed and as we made our way to the parking lot. I felt him walking a step behind me even though my instinct was to shadow him. Just like ordering Ethan to grip my neck, I leaned toward submission no matter the circumstance. I chastised myself, reminded of how badly I wanted to be strong. I turned to face Leo when I reached my car and suddenly felt weak at the sight of him. He took one bold step toward me and wrapped his arms around me.

Tears stung my eyes. His powerful embrace held my unstable pieces together.

"I love you," he whispered against my hair.

I let him hold me a beat longer then shrugged away from the strong arms I'd missed so much, wiping the tears that had spilled down my cheeks. Leo gazed down at me, boldly cupping one side of my face, holding my eyes. For the first time since he'd walked into the restaurant, I thought of his black gloves. I missed the feeling of his soft leather touch wiping away tears that sprang from intense pleasure.

"I used to think you were so beautiful when you cried. I'd take it all back if I could, Sloane. I'd do it all differently to make you happy again."

My head told me to tread lightly, go cautiously into every moment with him, but my heart encouraged me to forgive the mistakes he'd made and let go into the freefall his love offered. I pressed my lips together firmly and took one step back, forcing his hand to fall. "Goodnight, Leo."

Any other words and I would've burst into tears, thrown myself into his arms, and never let go. Leo nodded, gave a sad smile, and watched as I climbed into my car.

CHAPTER EIGHT

Leo

"Ready or not, here I come!" Barry's small voice rang out.

I couldn't keep the smile off my face as I stood shrouded by the thick drapes framing my sister's living room window. Hearing his footfalls nearing, I let out a light chuckle and huffed when his tiny arms wrapped around my knees through the curtains.

"I found you!"

I whipped the drapes to the side and feigned defeat, throwing my head back. "You're just too good," I said. "You sure you don't have some superhero advantage at hide and seek?"

"You're just bad at hiding, Uncle Leo," Barry laughed.

My mouth dropped, but I laughed at his brutal honesty, ruffling his brown curls as I passed him. "Let's have a snack. What do you want?"

"Ummm…pizza?"

"Pizza isn't really a snack, bud." I chuckled, glancing at the clock. "Your mom should be home soon. Maybe she'll let us get pizza for dinner. How about an apple until then?"

He nodded and I rinsed a bright red and green splotched apple from the bowl sitting on the counter before slicing it for him. The sound of the door made both of our heads turn. Barry raced toward Marie as she walked into the kitchen.

"Hey, Bear. Were you good for Uncle Leo?"

"He was great," I lied for him before he could.

I'd driven in early that morning so Marie could spend the day taking her real estate licensing exam. Despite how much he'd been telling me he missed me on the phone over the last few weeks, he was less than thrilled to see me when he woke up. Prior to the game of hide and seek, he'd fought me on just about everything from brushing his teeth to handing over the tablet when his screen time was up. It'd been a while since Barry and I had so much one-on-one time. I hadn't realized how quickly I'd lost the parental respect I once held. I supposed it was better that way though. He listened to Marie now.

I watched her bend to kiss the top of his head before she met me to take the plate of apple slices. Marie's hand rested between my shoulder blades as she smiled.

"Thanks again for coming," she said.

"Of course. How did it go?"

"I think I did really well," she replied, her smile splitting wider. "I'll know in a few days." Her tired eyes brightened a little as she slid the snack onto the placemat in front of Barry at the kitchen table.

"That's great," I said, watching Barry as he crunched on a piece of apple. "We were thinking we should probably celebrate you doing a good job on your test with some pizza. Right, Barry? Uncle Leo's treat."

"You don't have to do that," Marie said. "Don't you need to get back?"

I shook my head and waved a dismissive hand. "I'm off tomorrow. It's nothing."

She grinned and traded glances with her son. "Well then, we aren't going to turn down pizza. Let me go change. Order whatever you want."

The three of us ate on the couch while Barry's current favorite insufferable cartoon played—an added indulgence to pizza night. By the third episode, after the pizza was long gone, Barry snuggled up to my side and shut his eyes.

"I really appreciate you coming today," Marie said.

"You're welcome. I'm very proud of you."

She'd started her classes shortly after Sloane and I broke up and she shocked us all by actually following through. A new career awaited her, and it included newfound stability for Barry.

He shifted between us and Marie scooped him up into her arms. "I'll be right back," she whispered, carrying him off to bed.

I quickly changed the channel to the nightly news and by the time Marie came back, I'd cleared the paper plates and empty cups from the coffee table.

She sighed heavily. "You don't have to do all this, you know. You don't have to go back to the way things used to be. I've got it here. You know that, right?"

I nodded. "I do. I'm not sure what changed but it seems like you're doing really well. The house was so clean when I came in this morning, I almost didn't know what to do with myself all day." I laughed when Marie narrowed annoyed eyes at me. "Barry's doing awesome, too. He was showing me math today. You've really stepped up and it shows."

"Thanks." Marie smiled and rested her head on the sofa, a little laugh escaping. "You won't believe whose idea the real estate license was."

"I thought it was Mom..."

She pulled her lips tight and shook her head before lowering her tone to a whisper. "Warren."

Bile tickled the back of my throat and I looked away from my sister, scared of the darkness that seethed within me at the mention of his name. I heard her scoff and glanced at her again.

"I don't want to hear it, Leo. You can't deny that his suggestion was a good one. I'm working, I'm paying my bills, and I'm taking care of Barry so there's nothing left for you to worry about."

"Are you seeing him again?" I asked incredulously.

I saw her press her lips together and turn her head away. Defiantly.

"We have to talk about something," I started.

"No. We don't. What I choose to do with my personal

life is my business. Like I said, I'm doing just fine now. And isn't it important that Barry get to know his father?"

I rose from the couch and clenched my fists. I'd thought maybe Barry's behavior was only due to my absence, but maybe it was due to the presence of a new man. The idea of Marie letting Warren back into her life—into Barry's life—after his initial suggestion that she not have him at all made my blood run cold. And now, thinking about him waltzing back into my sister's home, knowing the deeper truth of his philandering ways and how he'd hurt Sloane too, caused rage to simmer in my gut.

"Do you think you know him? Do you think his wife is your only competition?"

"Leo, seriously, stop it. I won't hear it. I'm an adult and I know what I'm doing."

"He slept with Sloane."

Marie stiffened and her nose scrunched up as she glared at me. Slowly, she stood and stepped toward me, confusion swarming her expression. "What? Your girlfriend? That doesn't make any sense. Why would you say that?"

My chin dropped to my chest and I breathed heavily. "She used to live here. It seems crazy, but...Marie, that's why we broke up. She used to date Warren and I figured it out and didn't tell her. He broke her heart, just like yours. He stole time from her, just like he did to you. If I thought I hated him before—for the way he treated you and the way he dismissed Barry—now I loathe his existence."

Her eyes glossed over, but she never lost the look of confusion. "When?" she whispered.

I tilted my head toward the ceiling and sighed. "Remember how he just stopped calling? He'd moved on to Sloane. And God knows who else."

My chest ached as realization consumed me. I'd watched my sister suffer through Warren's disappearance with a small sense of happiness. She was devastated and while I hated that she had to suffer through the loss of him magnified by a bout of postpartum depression, I was relieved that Warren was seemingly out of our lives for good, aside from the sporadic checks he'd send in the mail. But the only reason that had happened was because of Sloane. Unbeknownst to me, I'd traded the freedom of my sister for the bondage of the woman I'd come to love just a few years down the road. And I was thankful for it. My heart sank at the look on my sister's face. She scowled and opened her mouth to speak but nothing came out.

"I'm sorry, Marie. But the fact of the matter is, he's a dog. I know it isn't my call but if I had my say, Barry would never see him. He's toxic."

A quick sniffle caused me to look at her closely, watching as tears claimed her and her shoulders shook.

"I'm so stupid," she cried.

I patted her arm and though it didn't come from my heart—it couldn't—I tried to feel for her. My insides were cold, though. I saw her anguish and only thought of Sloane. I hated myself for wishing he'd move on years ago. Not only had I held onto his secret for him, but I'd sent him her way. The hand I'd played in breaking her cut me deeply.

Even now, after our night together, talking and

attempting to mend our relationship, I knew the Dom drop from months ago lingered as waning depression. And with every revelation of Warren's disgusting reach into my life, I felt the part I'd played magnified by the sadness I saw in both Sloane and my sister. What could I have done to prevent this? How had I failed them both?

What penance did I owe to set things right?

Marie dragged her hands down her face and exhaled, wiping the tears she had shed. When she locked eyes with me, she shook her head. "I wish I could explain why I fell for him, Leo. I wish I understood the power he has over my emotions. I just can't. There's this part of me that knows he's awful and that he doesn't care about me or Barry, but then he makes me feel...I don't know...important—special— and I fall right back into it. He knows just what to say and it always seems real."

I squeezed her shoulder and cocked my head to one side, making her meet my gaze. "Just promise me you'll stay away from him."

Marie nodded but her tears welled once again, spilling down her cheeks as sobs claimed her. Pulling her toward me, I held her tightly as she wailed into my chest. Ice settled inside me and just as I trained all my energy on hating Warren, she spoke.

"Don't ever say you hate him again," she said, sniffing and pushing me away. Her fingers smudged her tears away as she crossed her arms and glared at me. "No matter what you think of Warren, your nephew is part of him and God help me if he ever sees the disgust on your face right now and understands it's directed at him. I can handle the shameful way you look at me, but I'll be damned if you ever set those eyes on my son. I know you're trying to help. I know you mean well. But you need to get off your high horse sometime soon and realize that we all make mistakes, Leo. Even you."

Brushing past me toward her room, I heard her angry sigh echo in my mind. I walked in a fog toward my coat, blinking to reach clarity. She'd never spoken to me like that and hearing her words, grasping how judgmental I'd always been of her, it was a wonder she hadn't clocked me instead of just yelling at me. She was right. I needed to come down from my high horse. It was about time I humbled myself, whether I was ready or not.

CHAPTER NINE

Sloane

I glanced at my phone and saw the text from Ethan, chewing on the inside of my cheek as I read it.

Ethan: *When can I see you again?*

I'd been avoiding him since I'd met Leo for dinner, once again feeling like I was cheating on him despite the fact nothing had changed between Leo and me. I'd used just about every excuse I could to keep him at bay, but he was losing patience.

Sloane: *Not sure. Job hunting has been my priority. I'll let you know.*

I wondered how he hadn't taken the hint yet. A little smile crossed my lips when I considered the fact that maybe I'd rocked his world.

Ethan: *We have a barista position open at B&B...*

I sighed. The opposite of what I needed. I didn't need to go right back to working for a man I'd slept with. A dark thought settled in my mind when I realized the last two jobs I'd had were that kind of arrangement. Just one more reason to steer clear of Ethan and keep my distance from Leo. I needed to take my own life back. It'd been my plan when I came to Salem in the first place, but Leo quickly derailed that plan with his black leather gloves and brooding blue stare.

"Who's blowing up your phone? Your Dom or your sub?" Bryon asked.

I shot him a look and slipped my phone into my purse without responding to Ethan's message. "A: I no longer have a Dom. B: I've never had a sub. And C: It's none of your goddamn business."

Bryon choked on a laugh and reared back, taking a sip of his coffee. "Reewr! Okay, you're clearly not in the mood. Sorry."

I huffed and popped the lid off my paper cup to let the mocha cool before I took a drink. I glanced around the coffee shop and felt the urge to rub my temples after snapping at my best friend.

I hated to admit it, but I was right back where I'd started. Restless nights followed by bitchy days, longing for naps to hide away from lingering thoughts of a man I didn't want to give a second thought to.

I could've sunk more time into Ethan, letting him try like hell to make me come, but getting off wasn't what I needed. I could've taken another step with Leo, continuing our conversation and slowly allowing him access to my life. But I was terrified I'd last all of five minutes before dropping to my knees.

"Sorry," I said. I knew I could confide in Bryon and as much as I hated to admit it he usually had good advice. "It's Ethan. He wants to see me again."

"And? Do you want to?"

"No. Yes. I don't know," I said with another heavy breath. "He's sexy. And nice—maybe too nice. But I don't know if I can keep up this whole Domme charade."

"What's a charade about it? I thought he was totally into it. And I thought you kinda liked it."

I gulped. I did kind of like it. Most of the time I felt myself wanting to order him to dominate me, but in the handful of moments that I didn't, I enjoyed the control. Even as mild as we'd played, there was something about the way it felt to be listened to and obeyed. But there was something not quite right about it. Ethan wasn't the right person. I didn't trust him in the same way I trusted...Leo.

"I just don't think it's a good idea to keep seeing him. I don't want him to get the wrong idea."

"You mean like the idea that you're available and not still in love with Leo?"

I shot daggers at Bryon, who quickly forced a cheeky smile. "I mean the idea that I'm interested in anything other than sex."

Bryon shook his head and took another sip of his coffee.

"What?" I growled.

"I don't know why I always have to be the one to spell it

out for you. You want so much more than sex, Sloane. Sex was your gateway drug with Leo."

My brow crinkled. "Gateway to what?"

"Intimacy."

He didn't elaborate. He didn't have to. I chewed the inside of my cheek and nodded absently as Bryon checked his phone for the time.

"I should get back to work," he said, standing.

I stood too, melting against his body when he pulled me into an unexpected hug.

"I don't mean to be a dick about it, but it's time to accept it, babe. It's time to let him back in and move on. Get this other shit out of your system and start putting the pieces back together."

I nodded and forced a smile. It was good advice, but I didn't know if I was ready to take it. Bryon's hand cupped my cheek and his eyes softened on me.

"You're right," I sighed. "You're a dick."

He laughed and pushed my shoulder before throwing his arm around me, leading us out the front door of the coffee shop.

———

Pulling into Melanie and Gabe's driveway, I forced myself to take a deep breath. The last time I'd been to their home had changed my life. Leo had guided me with a hand at my back, encouraging me to look down their halls and into their rooms, my own intrigue leading me to observe experienced players.

I lifted my hand to knock on the front door and replayed the conversation I'd had with Melanie a few days ago in my head. We'd met for a glass of wine after I'd spent the day applying for jobs around Salem. I relished the much-needed conversation and the rich red wine. After catching up on everything not related to S&M or Leo, I finally got bold enough to inquire after the subs who might be looking for a new Domme.

"Why don't you tell me what you're looking for and I can set something up?" she'd suggested.

What was I looking for? I had no idea. I already had Ethan on the hook; I should've just kept trying with him, but I'd continued to avoid his calls and texts. Sadly, I missed the coffee at Black and Brew most of all. I hadn't set foot in there in weeks. After meeting with Leo for dinner, I'd felt an ache begin to settle within me. I missed him. I missed what we had and who I'd been with him, as much as I hated to admit it. Calling Melanie was my attempt at doing exactly what Bryon had suggested—get the Domme thing out of my system and move on. I didn't know what that meant or what it would look like, but I knew I had to try.

Melanie assured me the setup would simply start as a chat and that whatever mystery suitor she found could meet me at her house—what she called neutral ground. And while that sounded reasonable, I hadn't thought about how quickly just the sight of her home would catapult me back to a moment in time with Leo. Sloane and Leo at the beginning of our story.

I'd done my best to describe what I wanted out of the experience. I wasn't into inflicting pain necessarily, and I wasn't a sadist the same way Leo was. I liked being in control. I wanted someone at my mercy. I wanted someone to give themselves to me completely, offering up their free will on a silver platter the way I had with both Warren and Leo. I wanted to know what it felt like to watch someone submit and know they'd done it for me.

She told me she'd contact some people and by the time she called me two days later, my feet were beginning to cool. I regretted bringing it up, let alone allowing her to reach out to someone on my behalf. I wasn't the kind of girl who'd fuck a stranger. Why on Earth had I even considered this?

As I waited for the door to open, a potentially new chapter waiting for me on the other side just as it had a few months back, I felt a little laugh trail through my mind. Here I was, shaking in my boots, and I would've fucked Leo that first night in the bookstore had he tried.

I was two people. Before Leo and After Leo.

The door swung open and Gabe smiled widely. I hadn't seen him since the night of the party, but I felt closer to him now having spent some time with his wife and learning more about their life together. He leaned in and pressed his cheek to mine, offering a kind greeting before ushering me inside.

His eyes grazed up and down my body, brows lifted,

and his lips formed an O, whistling low. "Sloane," he said. "You look fantastic. You certainly dressed the part."

I blushed and looked down at my clothes. I felt ridiculous, but his reaction—especially knowing his sub status—eased my mind a bit.

Bryon had helped me pick out the black lace bustier, pairing it with a black jacket and tight mini skirt. I rarely wore heels and I even more rarely wore anything showing cleavage. I couldn't recall the last time I put on something this revealing. Bryon had to convince me that a bustier wasn't just a glorified bra and even still, I questioned that logic. But as Melanie swept around the corner, looking gorgeous as ever in a white wrap dress, her eyes sparkled and I knew I'd made the right choice.

"You look amazing," she breathed, pulling me close.

I felt the sudden wave of worry wash over me. What had I gotten myself into? This guy could be anyone.

Melanie's hands came down on my shoulders and she forced my gaze to meet hers. "This is just to talk. You don't have to do anything tonight. He's just as nervous as you so don't worry."

I pushed a hand through my hair and sighed heavily, my pulse quickening. "Isn't this weird though? This isn't normal. I've never even been on a blind date before, let alone something like this."

Her hands smoothed down my arms, finally linking her fingers with mine, squeezing them gently. "It's unconventional, yes. But he recognizes that and so long as there's communication, I don't think—in fact, I know—he won't have a problem with unconventionality."

Her lips fought against a smirk and the moment I saw her exchange glances with Gabe, my stomach dropped. I took a step back and ripped my hands from hers, glaring at her.

I don't know why I hadn't thought of it sooner. Why didn't I expect this?

"Melanie," I hissed. I let my eyes move past her to where I assumed he was waiting. "Tell me you're not about to spring him on me..."

She reached for me, her face falling and her mouth twisting into a frown. "You don't understand. Just come inside. Keep that open mind you had a few minutes ago."

I snatched my arm away from her again and shot a look at Gabe. "Is it him? He's here?"

Gabe sucked in a tight breath and simply moved his eyes to his wife without a word. I covered my face with my hands and turned for the door. I'd never felt so stupid or gullible in my life.

"Sloane, please. It's just to talk, remember?"

"This is not what I wanted, Melanie." My voice rose and my lungs grew tight, anger stifling each breath. "How could you do this?"

"Don't be mad at her."

I shut my eyes at the sound of his voice in the distance. It still made me weak. Ethan's calls hadn't been the only ones I'd been avoiding. After meeting Leo for dinner, after the promises of starting over as friends and getting to know one another, I'd made every excuse not to see him for fear I'd lose sight of the friendship we'd embarked on and do what my heart and my hormones told me to do—drop to my weakened knees.

I looked over Melanie's shoulder. Dressed in a simple white t-shirt and jeans, the sight of Leo walking toward me made me furrow my brow. He looked completely unassuming. Casual but sexy as always. His eyes dragged up my body from my stilettos to the crest of my breasts shameless exposed by the goddamn bra I'd chosen to wear with only a jacket.

I turned from him and took a step toward the door, embarrassment and shame swarming my every thought.

"Please, Sloane," he said as he reached me, placing a hand on my forearm.

I spun, filled with sudden rage and a million hurtful words. But when I looked at him, he pulled back, his gaze moving to the floor. I took a moment to look him over, narrowing my eyes at the stark differences. He was more than unassuming. The plain clothes, his posture, his soft expression and averted eyes....

"What are you doing here?" I breathed.

Leo didn't look up and though I missed the sight of his penetrating blue irises, his response was enough to send a chill through me.

"I'm here for you, Sloane. I'm here to submit."

CHAPTER TEN

Leo

I kept my gaze on the ground and listened for the catch in her breathing. Making this plan with Melanie had been foolish and I knew it, but I wasn't going to lose her for good. I didn't stand a chance without her in my life. Without Sloane, I was a sad drunk, a shitty brother, and a less than stellar business owner. I'd been slacking at the store and Oliver knew it. He made excuses for me and let too much slide. I didn't even have it in me to be happy for him as he and Wendy planned their wedding and the impending birth of their child.

Then there was Marie. After I told her the truth, still fearful deep down that what I'd shared with her wouldn't be enough to keep her away from him, I'd been desperate to talk to Sloane and crushed when she avoided every attempt I made to contact her. When I reached out to Melanie and Gabe for advice, I hadn't expected the opening I was given.

Sloane was looking for a sub and she'd asked Mel to facilitate it.

The thought had only begun to cross my mind once I was rocked by guilt over the role I'd played in Sloane's unhappiness, before and after our relationship.

I owed her this. I owed her more than this.

Convincing Melanie to let me infiltrate her setup and be the sub waiting for Sloane had proved difficult, but once I explained my side of the story, she weakened. I'd all but begged her, trying my hand at the role with another Domme first. When she finally agreed, I felt sick. And it wasn't until I heard Sloane's furious voice in the other room that I knew I had to make her stay.

"What do you mean, you're here to submit?" she whispered.

I didn't look up from my shoes as I swallowed hard. It wasn't my nature, but I kept quiet and waited.

"You two are welcome to use the living room to chat. We'll get out of your way," Gabe said from my side.

Sloane huffed as Melanie and Gabe walked away. I slowly lifted my head and even though I met her stare, I held my breath.

Squinting at me, she gritted her teeth then huffed again as she pushed past me. I followed her to the living room and sat on the opposite end of the couch. She sat stiffly, and for a moment I worried my bold move would backfire and leave us more damaged than before.

"May I explain?" I whispered.

She scoffed. "Sure. But I think I know what you're doing. I'm not an idiot."

"And what do you think I'm doing?"

She glared at me, eyes narrowed and mouth firm. "For someone who doesn't allow 'topping from the bottom,' I have a pretty good idea that's what's about to happen here."

I swallowed and took a silent moment to gather my thoughts. My body moved to hers slowly and I slid off the sofa to crouch in front of her. Her eyes grew wide as I gently touched her thighs through the fabric of her skirt. I cursed myself for the boldness of my touch and moved my hands to grip hers where they lay in her lap. Kneeling before her, I stared at our clasped hands.

"I've proven I'm a selfish man. I need to show you that I can overcome that."

Her eyes softened but her brow remained tense as she stared at me. "Why?" she whispered.

"Because I want you to trust me again. I want to give you what you deserve—what you desire—and if this is what it takes, I'm willing."

"But you won't like it. What's the point if it doesn't satisfy you?"

I squeezed her hands firmly. "I get my pleasure from your pleasure—don't you see that? You're the key to my experience. I'm willing to do whatever it takes to please you," I said. "To earn your trust again. To offer my love in whatever way you need it."

Sloane licked her bottom lip and turned away, her eyes

welling with tears. "You make it sound so easy," she breathed with a disheartened laugh.

"Maybe it will be, maybe it won't be. But it's a step. Let me do this for you. If you're willing to try this for yourself—at least try it with me."

She met my gaze unexpectedly; all traces of her tears had disappeared. "And if I like it?" she started. "Then what?"

I heard her words as a memory. The evening at the bookstore when I'd slipped one of the more informative lifestyle books into her purse, urging her to brush up on the subject before tumbling down the rabbit hole with me. One corner of my mouth ticked up as I suddenly felt the absurdity of fear float into my stomach. She was about to give in, which meant I was about to submit for the first time in my life. While I couldn't imagine how it would make me feel, there wasn't another person in this world I'd rather bow down to.

"Who knows, Sloane? Maybe you'll make my life a carousel."

Her eyes lit with a touch of joy and a hint of relief at my jest. And as her chin rose after one steady breath, I watched the Domme in her emerge in the most subtle, sexy, unsettling way.

"I guess we should go over limits then."

CHAPTER ELEVEN

Sloane

Steeling myself with a breath, I sent him inside a room with instructions and closed the door so I could prepare myself. The sincerity in Leo's eyes when he'd suggested himself as my trial sub rocked me to my core. I still didn't know if I was ready for all of this. Even though it confused me, the idea of taking this leap with Leo at my side didn't scare me as much. It made it easier.

I turned the knob and walked into the dimly lit room. It was the same room we'd seen Melanie and Gabe playing in during the party months ago. An assortment of fetish furnishings sat around the room and a pegboard on the far wall holding every implement of punishment I could fathom. I sucked in a gasp when I locked gazes with the stoic lion on Leo's back. He stood facing the wall with his head down and his arms slack.

I drank in the sight of him and sighed, trying to will away my need for him and stir my dominance.

"Who told you to take off your shirt?"

The muscles in his back tightened but he didn't turn toward me. "I'm sorry, my love," he whispered.

The title sent a shiver through my bones. "Come over here," I demanded.

Leo turned. I traced the sharp edge of his jaw as he quickly locked eyes with me before lowering his gaze once more. With trembling fingers, I reached into the breast pocket of my blazer and pulled out the ladies' black leather gloves Bryon had gifted me. As I slid them on my fingers, I caught Leo's glance and the catch of his breath. Without warning, a quiet dark laugh fell from my lips.

"That's right," I said. "It's my turn."

I watched him smile then bite his lip, lowering his head again.

"Kneel."

Fire licked up my spine as Leo obeyed my order, dropping to his knees before me.

"Look at me."

The blue eyes that had once easily stunned me into submission softly rose to gaze expectantly at me. He swallowed hard and I watched him relinquish control in that moment. Satisfaction flooded me and warmed my blood. The sight of him waiting for my next command riveted me to the core.

My hand reached out, sheathed in soft leather, and threaded through the hair at his temples. With our eyes glued to each other, I stroked his head gently. But when darkness drifted into his stare and I saw his internal struggle, I gripped the thick black waves of his hair and yanked his head back. A growl rumbled through his throat and I scanned his face, trailing down to his jutting Adam's apple. I watched it bob as he swallowed, my instinct to dip low and let my tongue skate across it. I resisted.

"How do you feel?" I whispered in a barely audible tone.

His eyes were on me gently, his lips unmoving, but the stiffening of his jaw told me what I wanted to know. He was struggling, fighting the dominance aching within him to emerge.

My fingers loosened in his hair and I stepped away from him toward the table of tools. I felt my insides quiver. I was completely at a loss, untrained and naïve in the ways of a true Domme. My eyes swept over the instruments of pain and pleasure laid out on the pegboard and on the table beneath it. With one tentative hand, I reached for a familiar piece to examine. The long, gleaming silver handle felt lighter in my grasp than I'd expected and when I touched the end of it, I grinned. This was a different kind of Wartenburg wheel than Leo had once used on me. I pressed the tines against my leather-covered palm and watched as a row of five spiked tines rolled across making tiny indents.

I grabbed a silk rope lying to the side of the tools and walked back to Leo, still on his knees. Standing behind him, I leaned down and secured his wrists behind his back without so much as a word. Hearing the quick groan come from the back of Leo's throat, I felt myself hesitate at my next move.

"Tell me your safe words."

He breathed a little laugh and I saw his head drop. I kept my gaze tight on the tension between his shoulder blades, only drifting to his bound wrists once when he shifted and tugged on the restraints.

"Yellow to slow. Red to stop. Black to end."

"Good," I whispered as I lowered the spiked metal wheel to rest on the top of his right shoulder. He sucked in a gasp and swallowed thickly.

I rolled it across his flesh slowly at first, envisioning the feeling of the tines on my skin. Goosebumps flashed out on both of us at the same time. I didn't press the spikes down. I felt like teasing him, not hurting him. I rolled the tiny, tortuous tool down the back of his neck and along his spine, grinning unexpectedly when Leo shuddered.

"How do you feel?" I asked again.

"Powerless."

I dragged the sharp spiked wheel along his skin again then stepped around to see his face. I pushed down ever so slightly, watching the redness appear near his collarbone. I saw him wince and pulled the instrument away from his flesh. Leo's eyes flickered to mine, tightening when he focused on my face.

"If you were me right now, what would you do?"

Leo sighed and I struggled to read the expression on his face. His eyes dropped to the floor and he shook his head barely. "I don't know."

My breathing picked up speed and suddenly my neck grew hot. I stepped toward him, completely erasing any comfortable distance between us, and pressed the Wartenburg wheel into his pec, carving a C shape as I drew it downward.

"If I lied to you, betrayed your trust, kicked your world off its axis then begged for forgiveness and dropped to my knees—what would you do? Would you make it hurt? Would you lose yourself in the scene? Cross lines and push limits even if you knew no amount of pain inflicted on your sub could erase what you'd already felt?"

I looked at the way the metal teeth had pitted and reddened his skin before I zipped the wheel up his chest. He sucked in a breath through his teeth then gnashed them at me, glaring up to where I stood over him.

"If you want revenge this isn't the way to do it," he said. "Untie me."

I gulped and shut my eyes as I let the hand holding the wheel fall to my side. What the hell was I doing? I made my way around his body again but stopped the moment my hand reached out to loosen his restraints.

He didn't use a safe word.

"No," I replied. I swore I could feel his smirk on the air.

My feet led me to look at him once more and I saw the devilish smile I'd predicted. "Good girl," he whispered.

Lava trickled along my spine and pooled in my belly. My bones weakened at the sight of that look on his handsome face and those words dripping from his lips. "Shut up," I breathed and stepped toward him, gripping a fistful of his hair again, tugging his head back. I damned my heart for loving him and I damned my cunt for aching with need the moment his voice dropped to the assertive timbre I'd been silently wishing for.

"You want to know what I'd do?" he whispered. "I'd make sure you'd never remember a time when I wasn't inside you. I'd tell you that I love you because it's true. And then I'd fuck you like I don't because I know that's how you like it. If the roles were reversed—if you hurt me how I hurt you...I'd make positive that my kind of punishment—the kind that leaves you wet, aching, crying, and spinning like a fucking hurricane—is the only penance I'd ever make you pay."

My mouth dropped and my throat tightened, the feeling of cotton engulfing my tongue. His words rolled around in my mind as my hand relaxed in his hair and smoothed to stroke his cheek. I leaned over him, one hand snaking behind his back. I tugged at the quick knot securing his wrists until he was free, then I turned and headed for the door. I couldn't do this.

CHAPTER TWELVE

Leo

"Sloane, wait," I called out. I shook the loosened rope from my hands and rose to chase after her.

She stopped near the door and I reached for her gloved hand. The feel of the material was unsettling; my stomach pitched when I realized she wasn't turning to look at me.

"You have to quit running," I said with a sigh.

She yanked her hand back. "I don't have to do anything."

I heaved a breath and my shoulders dropped a little. My hand rose to scrub over my eyes as I pinched them closed. "This wasn't my plan. I shouldn't have said those things. I didn't come here to trick you...to top you. It's just my nature. I can't help myself around you. You should've gagged me," I said with a halfhearted laugh.

Sloane turned carefully and pinned me with her darkened eyes and firm jaw.

"I can do this. I swear I didn't mean to—"

She cut me off, boldly clamping her hand over my mouth, her fierce gaze locked with mine. Her other hand palmed my chest and pushed me back. Guiding me, she shoved me steadily backwards into the room, turning until my legs knocked into the large wingback chair near the corner. With determined hands, Sloane coaxed me to sit. I stared up at her in awe, watching as she walked over to Melanie and Gabe's menagerie of toys and play items. I wondered what she'd choose and if she'd make me pay for my words with pain.

Sloane slinked back over to me with a piece of silk fabric in one hand. With caution in her eyes, she held the two-inch wide white strip taut between her fists and moved it over my lips. The feeling of the cool material brushing my mouth made me instinctively open. Her lips flickered into a quick smile that faded the moment she pushed the gag between my teeth. She tied it at the base of my neck, the slight padding of my overgrown hair the only thing keeping it halfway comfortable.

I watched with bated breath, biting down on the silk as her fingers worked open the button of my jeans then the zipper. She tugged, and I lifted my hips enough for her to shuck my pants down to my ankles. I didn't dare move my hands without her permission. Sloane skimmed her slender fingers over my bare chest, her eyes intently watching the connection of black leather and my increasingly heated flesh. I felt my breath quicken.

"You never let me touch you like this," she mused under

her breath, letting her thumbs dust over my nipples then swipe down the ridges of my stomach. Air continued to raise and lower my torso while she loomed over me.

"Er ne're—"

She immobilized me with a glare and a wicked smile I hardly recognized on her when I tried to speak around the gag. "Shush," she whispered, leaning down to kiss the corner of my mouth.

A jolt of electricity rippled through me as I took notice of the keen level to her voice and the ease of her movements. She'd settled in. Wide-eyed and almost breathless, I watched as her hands played along my skin until she finally reached my stiffening cock, gripping me without hesitation through my boxers. Her sultry mouth curved when I hardened and grew in her hand, a little noise slipping past the gag when I took a moment to appreciate how the role seemed to suit her. That the strong, confident look in her temptress eyes excited me. It didn't matter that my hands were free; she had me bound by looks alone.

She inched her skirt up around her hips, revealing her pussy to me for a split second before settling herself on my lap, straddling my dick. A sigh rushed out of me as she bucked against me once.

My hands twitched to touch her. I held out as long as I could, but after a few more teasing humps, her heated pussy grinding against me through a layer of cotton, I reached out for her hips. Her head fell back and a moan dripped from her lips as I clutched at her thighs, pulling her to me firmly.

I shut my eyes and helped rub her against me until she

snatched my wrists in her hands and pinned them over my head, pressing them into the back of the chair.

"Behave yourself," she reprimanded.

At first, I gulped and resisted the urge to struggle against her, knowing I could easily gain control with my strength. But as her gaze softened and a smile tipped up her lips...I melted.

I hadn't seen her happy in so long, it nearly brought tears to my eyes. I'd missed her so fucking much. I shook away the sudden emotion and relaxed under her touch again. She kept my wrists captured while the other hand snaked between us to pull my cock from my shorts. I sighed as she lifted herself off me only to lower back down, enveloping my body with her wet heat.

"Uhnph," I croaked around the silk tie in my mouth, damp from saliva and surely punctured by my molars. I gritted my teeth as she began to ride me as I sat helpless, getting fucked by the most beautiful woman I'd ever known.

She let go of my hands and unbuttoned the jacket she wore, tossing it behind her. I ached to reach out and cup her tits with my bare hands—a privilege I'd only taken advantage of a few times. As though she'd heard my inner desires, she touched herself through the black lace bra, throwing her head back with a noise that was half bliss and half agony.

Her pussy tightened around me as she writhed in my lap, lost to unbridled craving and hedonism—a true Dominant taking what pleased her.

I thought I felt her getting close when she pushed her hands through her hair as if frustration suddenly tormented her. She leaned in close, dipping her head in the crook of my neck, allowing me the pleasure of inhaling the scent of her hair. Hot breath tickled my throat and a groan consumed me when her tongue lapped at the skin below my ear. She kissed the place and I realized I'd never allowed her this kind of freedom with me before. I liked having control over her sexually, but I liked this too. I liked witnessing the power behind her every move and I liked watching the wheels turn in her mind as she decided what to do next. I didn't care for the gag and I didn't like how the rope had felt around my wrists when she had me kneeling on the floor, but I wasn't against this game we were playing. In fact, as her teeth began to nip at my throat and her lips sucked the flesh harder and harder as she rode me, a thought infiltrated my mind. I wanted to wear Sloane's bruise. I wanted her to suck on my flesh, stippling it with a pattern of purple and red flecks, marking me so the world knew I belonged to her. I wanted her to mark me.

I sighed when she ducked her face toward the opposite side of my neck, capturing the sensitive skin there. I nearly lost it when she gave a bite after drawing my flesh roughly between her suctioning lips.

"You like that?" she breathed in my ear. She leaned back to look in my eyes and I tried to tell her wordlessly. Yes, I liked it. I loved it. I loved her. I didn't care who was on top as long as we were one. Inside her was where I belonged, no matter how our bodies were arranged.

She let go of a huff, unknown frustration painting her face once more. Her hands slid to the back of my head and she released me from the gag. Shifting my jaw, I licked my lips and silently thanked her for freeing me.

Her movements slowed and I could tell something had shifted between us. I watched her fingers reach out to touch the spots on my neck she'd greedily attacked. I wondered how noticeable the marks would be by morning.

"Do you love me?" she whispered.

I boldly let my hands slide up her thighs again, not grabbing but simply connecting with her in one more place. "Yes," I said. "I love you, Sloane."

Her eyes never met mine. They swam from my bruised throat to my chin to my shoulders and finally down to the place where our bodies continued to meet, rocking slowly together in a rhythm that left us both pleased but not pushed over the ultimate edge.

"Will you do what I say?"

I breathed a light laugh. What did she think I'd been doing? "Of course, my love. Whatever you want."

I never thought I'd say the words. I never thought I'd allow myself to be topped and I knew it wasn't about the role itself, it was strictly about Sloane. I wouldn't be this person for anyone else. She and she alone could rule me for a time.

She swallowed hard and panted, as though her breath didn't come easily. Her eyes darted around anxiously, and she clawed at her neck before reaching around to unhook and remove her bustier. Something had changed. She was unsettled to the point I nearly called out a safe word to check in on her, even though I knew that would potentially ruin the good thing we had going. Finally, her eyes locked with mine and she breathed deeply, sinking into the same black hole I'd been waiting for her in.

"Pin me down," Sloane whispered.

I tensed but I didn't ask her to repeat herself. My breath caught in my chest as it slowly dawned on me what she was commanding.

"Hold me down and tell me again that you love me," she said before leaning into my ear, her breath forcing a shudder to claim me, "and fuck me like you don't."

Without a second to breathe, I rose from the chair, one arm cinched around her waist. I laid her gently on the floor and instantly felt her body relax. I shoved my boxers off, casting them aside as I lowered myself on top of her. One hand gathered her wrists and trapped them above her head while the other forced one thigh out as wide as she could stretch, a deep groan echoing out of her as I drove my dick deep inside her.

I fucked her hard, wildly thrusting in the way I'd been dreaming about, the sound of her euphoric cries only urging me deeper. I let go of her wrists and gripped her chin, making her look at me.

"I love you," I growled.

She moaned and I took the opportunity her parted lips presented and kissed her hard, shoving my tongue in her mouth and eliciting another guttural noise. Her hands clutched my head, keeping my lips against hers so she could suck my bottom lip in between her teeth. I let her keep ahold of me, shivering when she bit down on my lip. Only then did I realized we were on even playing ground. I didn't know who was making the rules at that point. Had she bottomed from the top or had I topped from the bottom? My Domme had commanded me to be her Dom...

Sloane's gloves raked through my hair before her hands fell easily above her head, leaving her in that vulnerable position I loved. I dropped my head and sucked hard on the flesh around her nipples, determined to mark her as mine the way she'd graffitied my skin with the color of her affection.

I felt her begin to shiver underneath me as I tongued her nipples, sucking them deeply then flicking them gently, alternately, teasingly. The noise she released made me look up. I caged her in with my arms pressed into the floor on either side of her head. My hips pinned her down while I fucked her harder, every thrust creating a grunt from me and a moan from her. Our eyes locked and warmth flooded me. It wasn't just my orgasm about to overwhelm me, it was her. I could see in her eyes how she'd changed now that I had the power. Since she'd handed the reins to me, her skin flushed differently, her lips softened and her eyes glistened while love, adoration, and awe sat deep within them.

"I love you, Sloane," I whispered.

She licked her swollen lips and grinned, reaching for one of my hands and settling it on her throat before she spoke. "I love you, too, Sir."

I tightened my grip on her neck, knowing exactly what she wanted and how she wanted it. I didn't realize how much I'd missed the feeling of her clenching around me until I felt it one more time. I never wanted to be without her. I was bound to her in way that felt needy and primal and absolutely terrifying. As I continued to look into her eyes, pumping closer to release, I knew that while clinging desperately to her flesh, I was truly bound to her soul.

CHAPTER THIRTEEN

Sloane

His arms around me as I slowly came down from the heaven he'd gifted me felt so right. Everything about what had just transpired felt as though it was exactly meant to be. I loved him. I'd never felt the infinite bliss Leo elicited with anyone else. As his arm cinched my naked body tighter to his, my blazer and his white t-shirt splayed strategically over our bodies to keep a little warmth, I sighed.

"That's the first time I've come in months," I admitted.

"Seriously?"

Leo's eyes blinked open slowly and his brow dipped in the center as I nodded. Part of me wanted to confess my tryst with Ethan—get it out in the open right away—but I couldn't. I knew I'd sully the joyful moment before too long, but I didn't want it to be with that information. I wondered what Leo would think of me if he knew.

"Well, we have some lost time to make up for then, don't we?" he crooned, sliding one hand down my naked hip.

"We're more than this, right?" I whispered to the air between us. There, joyful moment ruined by my over-analytical, negative bullshit.

"Do you really have to ask that?"

I swallowed thickly. I didn't. But fear constantly waved in and out of me when it came to him—when it came to love...happiness.

"What are you so afraid of?"

My eyes closed, my lungs filling with the breath we shared between us. Honesty and communication had always been what we lacked—what we avoided and carelessly overlooked—thinking sex could be our language. As much as our brand of sex built intimacy, we lacked an integral part of a healthy relationship. We needed to change that if we were moving forward from here.

"When I lost my parents, my entire world changed in a second," I said quietly. "One minute I was happy and surrounded by love and the next I was alone and no one could fix it. I blamed myself for their deaths in the most ridiculous ways. Like if I hadn't borrowed my mom's curling iron the week before she would've found it where it belonged, and then they wouldn't have been five minutes late when they headed out. Or if I hadn't distracted my dad one entire weekend with helping me prep for a chemistry test, he wouldn't have forgotten to book the limo company he'd used before and they wouldn't have ended up in the one that killed them. I pushed my sister away for years.

Bryon's been my only close friend since college. Probably because I'm so miserable no one wants to be around me." I sighed heavily and stared down at Leo's bare sternum. "And as an adult I've made a habit out of choosing men who were unavailable, jobs that were easy to leave, and keeping people at arm's length...because I don't want to lose anything again. And if I never really have it to begin with...."

My eyes wet with tears but a halfhearted laugh snuck out of me as easily as a breath. Just when I thought I needed to call my psychiatrist, Dr. Keith, a little rough play with Leo was all I needed to have a breakthrough.

"I wasn't unavailable," he whispered.

"Yes, you were. You like being a mystery," I said. "One big walking secret—quiet and brooding and cagey at times. Even when I was falling in love with you, I didn't know you. You were a code I could never crack."

Leo's eyes closed. "We can fix this."

"I know we can. But not with sex." I gestured to the playroom around us, juxtaposing the way we cuddled one another lovingly. "We can't play our problems away."

"Of course. We'll go out, we'll stay in, we'll talk. Reconnect. You know I'll do anything." His hand drew delicate circles on my lower back as he held me close. "But I need you, Sloane."

I stared at him without a word, thinking of all the reasons I knew why I needed him too.

"There's a storm in your soul the same as mine, Sloane. Maybe you never felt like you knew me, but I've always believed I could see into your mind. I know there's a voice in your head that tells you you're less than. The same voice told you that you were to blame when your parents died and the voice that told you a man like Warren was as good as you deserved. If that voice isn't under control, you start to believe it." He reached out and cupped my cheek, pulling my body closer to his, erasing the space between our naked bodies, pressing me against the warmth of his bare flesh. "Let mine be the voice that controls you," he whispered against my cheek before kissing my temple and moving to my ear. "Let me punish you and rule you the way that voice inside does. Let me embody the darkness within you so you don't have to, my love."

My eyes fluttered closed and I moaned as his soft tongue flicked gently across my earlobe. He was right about me. He'd always been able to read me so effortlessly.

"Let me be your only demon."

The whisper against my flushed skin scattered goose-bumps over my body and sparks shot off in my mind. When I reached for his chin to guide him to my lips, I realized I was still wearing my black leather gloves. A wave of calm washed over me as I remembered what he'd said when we first began. The submissive was the strong one.

I gripped his chin and led him to kiss me. His tongue brushed against mine and he rolled me onto my back, slowly moving my arms above my head before painting my body with the sweetest touch he'd ever offered. As his kisses traveled south, I closed my eyes and succumbed to the power he wielded over me, reveling in the bliss that enveloped me when I accepted the role I preferred.

———

Before I pushed through the door to Calloway Books, I stared down at the screen of my phone and bit my lip. It was the fifth text in as many days.

Ethan: *I keep thinking about your beautiful face. Hope you're doing okay.*

The innocent bystander in all of this was Ethan. He hadn't known the kind of hurricane he was stumbling into when he started crushing on me. And I was cruel enough not to tell him. Even crueler, I grabbed him by the hand and yanked him into the eye of the storm with me. I knew I'd have to face him sooner or later now that the tides had turned.

The front door of the store swung open and I jumped as Leo popped his head out. "Hello, beautiful," he greeted with a beaming smile.

I grinned, the heat behind his gaze reminding me of our long-extended night locked in Gabe and Melanie's spare room. "Hi," I said.

"So, I promise I'm still good for dinner," he rushed, "but the computer just crashed and Wendy is puking and Oliver is holding her hair back or something. I'm just...a little swamped. Just for a few more minutes though."

Words spewed out of him as he clung to the door and

cringed, prepping me as though waiting for him for a few minutes—even a few hours—would upset me.

"Don't worry. I'm not going anywhere," I reassured him.

His face softened into a pleased smile before he nodded down the road. "You should go grab us some coffees. It's been a hell of a day, but I plan to stay up all night with you so...hit me with a double shot?"

I considered the text in my hands. He'd gestured toward Black and Brew. Leo stepped down onto the sidewalk with me, putting his hands on my elbows before looking over his shoulder where someone had just approached the counter.

"Sorry," he said with a sigh. "This is me desperately trying not to screw up our second first date."

I smiled to ease his worry. "You're not screwing up. I'll go get us some drinks and we'll stay as long as we have to. I'll even jump behind the register if you need me."

Leo's hand reached out and slid under the hair at my neckline. He pulled me to him gently and pressed a kiss on my forehead. When he released me, I opened my eyes, realizing I'd shut them to enjoy the feel of his lips on my face. I smiled again and tried to cover the beam I felt the need to shine at him for the sweetness of the exchange, then turned toward Black and Brew. Only then did I feel my stomach flutter with the fear of seeing Ethan and the guilt of what I'd have to say to him.

I pushed through the door and breathed in the glorious scent of rich coffee and sweet syrups. Hurrying to the counter, I placed our drink order and took a spot by the pickup area with my arms folded. Maybe he'd be off or in the back doing managerial things. Maybe I'd be in and out before he even noticed me.

The warm hand I felt on my shoulder blade sent a shiver through my gut. "Hey, you," Ethan said.

"Hey." My voice was weak and foreign on my tongue. Scanning his face, I felt sick. I never should have let myself be so reckless as to fall into bed with Ethan. He was kind and gentle and probably the right kind of guy for me or any woman lucky enough to catch his attention. But he wasn't what I wanted, and he definitely wasn't who I needed.

"You, uh, haven't been around lately. Been back in Blacksburg?"

I gulped and shook my head, a weak and painfully sad smile touching my lips. My hand rose to brush hair back from my face and I sighed.

"Ethan—"

"House blend, double shot and a chocolate mousse mocha for Sloane," the barista behind the counter called out.

"One for you and one for...?" Ethan started as he watched me grab the two drinks.

I sighed again. "Leo."

A pained smiled curved his mouth and he gave a slight nod.

"We ran into each other and just sort of—"

He held up a hand and shook his head, the same soft, sad smile on his lips. "It's okay. I get it."

"Ethan, I'm sorry."

"Don't be." His tender brown eyes swept over my

features and amazingly, I didn't see an ounce of anger. "Are you happy, Sloane?"

I gulped. In the past year, I'd asked myself that question more times than in my entire life. With everything that had changed, the back and forth with Leo and where we seemed to be headed now, I was surprisingly feeling happier than I had in ages. Our lines of communication were clearing and it was very apparent that Leo was determined for us to do things right this time.

"Yeah, I am," I said. Though Ethan had never felt like more than a way to scratch an itch, I felt guilty for the way I'd used him. He'd simply helped me get something out of my system and distracted me while my love for Leo festered and eventually took over, unable to stay quiet. But Ethan didn't deserve to be used and strung along.

"Good," Ethan replied. "You deserve to be happy. I guess I'll see you around."

My heart sank and I nodded, knowing there was nothing else I could say to make it right. I hoped Ethan found a woman he could make happy and who'd fall for him the way I could've, had my life been different.

I smiled at the young family as they headed outside with their bulging bags of books then sighed, remembering how carefree my life had been back when I was working at the store.

Leo popped his head out of the office, looking more

exhausted than an hour ago, but emerging. "You ready to get out of here?"

I grinned and nodded. I let my eyes travel up and down his body, wondering if this date would end in bed.

"Where should we eat?"

I chuckled under my breath. I wasn't used to this version of Leo—the one offering me choices and deferring to my opinion. Shrugging, I gazed up at him and melted under his touch as he settled his strong hands on my waist.

A heavy breath coated with lust passed his lips as he looked at me. "I'd love to just lock the door and take you upstairs, you know." We both grinned and I felt my cheeks grow hot. "But I can't," he said. "I won't keep letting sex distract me from being the best man I can be for you. So we're going out on a date and I'm going to stare at you from across the table and let your voice hypnotize me for as long as you'll allow it."

"No, you won't," I replied.

Leo's brow jumped then a quick smirk curved his mouth.

"You're coming to my place. To cook with me."

His eyes softened as he lowered his lips to kiss me gently. "Of course, my love."

I turned from the stovetop where the sauce base had begun to simmer, my eyes landing on Leo's back as he chopped vegetables in silence. Biting my lip, I took in the sight of him, relaxed and at ease in my space. I felt my words brimming inside.

"What did you think of...of submission?"

I'd been wanting to ask him since the moment we both fell back down to earth in Melanie and Gabe's playroom, but we hadn't discussed it. I was done being afraid to ask what he was thinking. Transparency had been something he alluded to offering way back when he gave me his medical records, yet I'd never pushed the issue further than that.

Leo turned slowly and rested back against the kitchen counter, his arms folded over his broad chest. "I didn't hate it."

I flicked my eyes to the ceiling then met his stare again with a smirk. "Care to elaborate?"

His blue gaze narrowed on me non-threateningly. "I liked the challenge. And it proved to me how much I trust you. I've never found a Dominant woman to be sexy before, but you changed that. To know what you've been through, how much you've grown...it made me proud to see you take control. Of course, I was happy to have you submitting to me in the end. But, like I said, I didn't hate it."

I pressed my lips together hiding a smile. "Does that mean you'd try it again?"

Leo looked at the floor for a moment, then at me. In a few quick steps, he was in front of me, clouding my senses with the fragrance of his cologne and the sound of his breathing, towering over me.

My eyes flicked up and down his sturdy body, remembering in a few flashes every time he'd pleasured me. When I wet my lips, he put his hands on my waist and slowly skimmed up my ribs through my shirt, feeling the way my body tensed then calmed under his powerful touch. As his strong hands slid to my hips, I watched in awe as he lowered to his knees before me, never letting his palms disconnect from the curves of my body. Leo gazed up at me, ultimate sincerity in his eyes as his hands traced the backs of my thighs.

"I'm committed to making this work. Making you love me. Making you happy. Whatever it takes, my love."

Suddenly, emotion overwhelmed me and my eyes misted with tears. Leo stood and pulled me against his chest.

"Don't cry."

I sighed, never letting the tears materialize, though his sincerity and love had moved me. "I'm not. I'm just happy. I missed you so much. I never wanted to walk away but I was so angry at you."

"I'm so sorry," he whispered against the top of my head. His hand swept tenderly up and down my back.

"Me too."

We breathed in unison, the tension in my shoulder blades lessening with every exhale we shared. When the timer rang out a signal that it was time to add the next ingredients, I gently tugged away from him.

I could feel his eyes lingering on me as I stirred the chopped veggies into the simmering liquid, topping it off with a bay leaf before covering it. When I turned back to him, he smiled. It seemed so strange now to think of the many versions of him I loved. The strong, silent man, the firm Dominant, the gentle lover, the reluctant submissive. They weren't all equal, but they were all Leo and he was someone I wanted, any way.

"Be my date to Oliver's wedding."

I smiled and felt my heart squeeze tight in my chest, an involuntary expression of glee rather than anxiety. "Yes, Sir," I replied, watching his eyes darken with lust.

CHAPTER FOURTEEN

Leo

Although I'd knelt before Sloane numerous times since our first reversed scene, when I dug my fingers into the flesh of her thighs and sucked hungrily at her, there was no way in hell I was her sub. Her throaty calls and begs for mercy gave me every ounce of the control over her body that I craved.

"Say please," I commanded, and she obliged, moaning and muttering her best manners over and over again while I refused to let up. Her limbs shook and I grinned, riding it out with her, nothing but joy inside me knowing I'd rewarded my good girl the way she liked best.

Resting my face against her inner thigh, I blew a cool stream of air onto her and felt her shiver while she squealed and playfully pushed me away. Sloane looked down at me, sparkling eyes lost in ecstasy, and smiled sleepily. I dragged a hand over my chin and kept my temple connected to the heat of her body, a smile consuming me as well.

Her hand came to pat my head and her eyes fluttered closed softly as she muttered, "Good boy."

A laugh cracked out of me and I raced up her body from the position I'd been in, twisted between her legs, half-kneeling off the side of her bed. Gripping her forearms, I pinned her into the mattress and bit the pulsing flesh of her throat teasingly.

"Are you trying to make me laugh or are you itching for punishment?"

She chuckled huskily and fought against my grasp as I shifted my hands to her elbows and tightened my fingers around her.

"Ah-ah," I said, nipping at her earlobe once gently and then again with enough force to make her whine.

"We should start getting ready," she said.

Rolling my eyes, tightening my grip, and offering a firm gaze that told her I wasn't falling for that one, she relaxed beneath me once and for all. I dragged my nose along her jaw and kissed her softly, loving the way she melted under my body—under my rule. I, too, weakened in the moment, letting my hands slide from her elbows to her breasts then to brush her bare abdomen as it trembled.

Nuzzling her and letting the feeling of her body intoxicate me, I hummed a noise that showed my hand.

She laughed. "You love it when I'm a little brat, don't you?"

I pushed up on my palms and smirked at her. "Maybe."

Sloane's hand moved between us without hesitation, landing on my cheek as she gazed up at me fondly. "Are you keeping this?"

I shook my head slightly, confused, before I realized she was talking about my beard. I stroked it once myself and flashed her a grin. "I don't know. You don't like it?"

Her hand petted the thick, dark hair that had grown out of my depression and remained due to my complacency. She looked me over and something unnamable settled in her stare. "It's not for me to decide," she mused, the lingering submission in her tone nearly making me hard.

"But..."

"But I like you the way I met you," she said. She traced the facial hair and dragged her fingers down my chin to my Adam's apple, the bold touch causing me to gulp. "I like watching the muscles in your jaw firm up when you look at me. I like seeing the veins in your neck pulse when you're serious—when you tell me what to do."

Her fingers had trailed to my sternum. The tone of her voice made my blood react, warming my body from the inside out, lacing fire through me from my heels to my heart.

We'd settled back into our relationship, but it wasn't quite the same. We'd made love and gone on a few dates, remembering what it was like to be easy with each other, but we hadn't had a true scene since the night I first yielded to her at Gabe and Melanie's house. Every sexual encounter we'd shared since then had traces of our power struggle because neither of us would ever rise to the role of top or surrender to the role of bottom.

She cleared her throat and I realized I'd been staring at her in silence, contemplating the new dynamic between us and whether I had the strength to sink to my knees for her again.

"We should go," she whispered. "I need a shower."

I nuzzled her neck and drew in the aroma of her skin, nothing more than the scent of her arousal between us. "Stop wearing perfume," I rasped against her throat.

She moaned in response, half questioning and half in instant agreement.

"I like smelling the way you change when I'm around. Your body reacts to me in the subtlest ways."

Sloane pushed up and I allowed her to move me off her as she smiled softly, pulling the sheet to her chest. "Lose the beard and I'll toss my perfume."

I laughed at the challenge, as though I wouldn't do anything she asked of me. But this new facet to her, the no-nonsense, strong-headed woman who no longer feared the sound of her own voice, only made me love her more. I loved this Sloane in a new way. I wanted her differently. And of course, I'd obey her without much convincing.

I felt Sloane's hand slide between my shoulder blades and I turned to see her smiling, bathed in the blue cast of the dark aquarium. Our eyes drifted in unison to the massive glass enclosure where hundreds of brightly colored fish swam. Elizabeth cried in the distance. I saw Bryon rifling through the black backpack they'd brought with them nervously as Craig bounced her, trying his best to console the baby. The noise of a crying child still tugged at my heart, leftover instinct from Barry's infancy.

"She okay?"

"The shark scared her. Well, Bryon actually scared her by talking about the shark eating her," Sloane said with a light laugh and a shake of her head.

Bryon offered his daughter a stuffed giraffe that seemed to instantly calm her. Her little hands clutched the animal tightly under her chin and she sniffed as Bryon placed a hand on her head, smoothing her barely-there wisps of brown hair. Craig smothered a smile at his husband and set Elizabeth back down on the ground. The two men watched their daughter toddle toward the same glass Sloane and I stood in front of.

I crouched down beside her and grinned. "Aren't they pretty?"

She stared at me the way she had every time I spoke to her during our outing to the Blacksburg Aquarium—with a shy smile and then a giggle. I pointed to the orange and white striped fish I knew Barry would've dubbed Nemo and told her it was called a clownfish, to which she babbled back at me, "Fishy."

"See, Bry, point out the cuddly ones to the child. The pretty ones. The ones that star in Disney movies, not horror flicks," Craig teased.

I laughed but couldn't take my eyes off Elizabeth and her wonder as her gaze swam with the fish in front of her. A yawn claimed her and she squeezed her giraffe tighter before blinking sleepily and turning to me with a glossy stare.

"Home," she mumbled.

With a chuckle, I glanced up at Bryon, Craig, and Sloane. "I think she's done."

"All done," Elizabeth said, reaching up for Craig.

Craig lifted her into his arms and shot Bryon a look. "Gift shop though?"

Bryon rolled his eyes and nodded as we all headed to exit through the obligatory gift shop. Elizabeth was asleep on Craig's shoulder as Bryon begrudgingly stepped up to pay for the stuffed shark she'd picked out all on her own. By the time we found our cars in the parking lot, the sun was painting the sky pink and orange.

Bryon shook my hand and hugged me while Craig strapped Elizabeth into her carseat. "Good to see you guys. Thanks for coming to our side of town this time," Bryon said before eyeing Sloane at my side. "I'm glad it worked out."

He reached for Sloane and hugged her as Craig clapped me on the shoulder with a smile. "She may not be the biggest talker, but I think you left an impression on Sleeping Beauty," he said, hooking his thumb toward the car where Elizabeth continued to snooze.

"She's a sweetheart. Any time you need a babysitter, we've got you covered," I replied.

My chest tightened when I realized the boldness of my offer as Craig looked to Sloane with raised brows. She pressed her lips together, looking between me, Craig, and Bryon as my suggestion hung in the air.

"Sure do," she said, barely missing a beat.

"Well, you two would certainly make a good team of it…" Craig commented, a grin curving his mouth.

Sloane and I exchanged a look. A strangled laugh. And then a smile.

We said our last goodbyes then climbed in my car to make the drive back to Salem. As I buckled my seatbelt, I looked over at Sloane and caught her absently smiling.

"Maybe we would…" I whispered.

She met my eyes, the lingering smile softening her lips as they parted. I watched her suck in a breath. "What?"

One corner of my mouth kicked up in a smirk. Bratty girl. She knew exactly what I was implying.

"Maybe we'd make a good babysitting team. Maybe we'd be good at…taking care of a child together."

She didn't respond with anything other than a smile and my stomach pitched with worry, wondering if she was thinking of Warren. Of Barry and his other child—and the child he'd denied her. If my foolish sister continued to see him and make him a part of Barry's life, then Warren would remain a part of the Calloway family even tangentially. And if I had plans to make Sloane a part of the Calloway family then he wouldn't be gone from her life either. My throat tasted of bile as I considered the reaction she might have to what I was about to tell her, but I couldn't suppress it. I wouldn't lie or omit the truth any longer.

"I need to tell you something."

Her dark brows rose expectantly and the urge to lie simmered within me, fighting its way out. I resisted. With my hands on the wheel, not driving, the car not even turned on yet, I glanced past her and saw Bryon and Craig pull away.

I sighed. "I told my sister."

The look on her face surprised me. It was more resigned than I'd imagined and while she didn't look angry, I saw a hint of shame in her expression.

"What did she say?"

"She was confused."

Sloane nodded barely and my tongue swelled in my mouth as I held onto to the words I knew I needed to say.

"She's seeing him again."

She shook her head, breathing a harsh laugh. Acid raged in my gut. Sloane lifted her fingers to her forehead, her thumbs connecting with her jaw as she scrubbed at her face. Another dark curse of a laugh escaped and I gulped.

"He's still married..." she said, staring the hem of her shirt picking gently at the fabric.

"She knows."

"And he's fucking some twit who owns a bakery and looks like she's seventeen."

"What?" I growled, shifting in my seat toward her.

Her hands covered her face completely again then dragged down to her chin as she breathed deeply. Light bounced off her small diamond stud earrings peeking out from behind her burgundy hair. "I ran into him. He was with this girl and...then he said he missed me. He asked me out. God..."

I wanted to ask her a million questions. Where did she run into him? What did he say to her? Did he touch her? But as my mind raced and my hatred for Warren Barrett rooted deeper in my soul, I bit the inside of my cheek and stayed quiet.

"Do you know what I just can't get over?" she mused. "That the sweetest little boy—your nephew—is half him. I can't hate him because I know somewhere inside of him is a tiny part of the little boy he helped to create. But something ruined him a long time ago."

"I hate him. He is destructive and vile and given the chance, I'd—"

Her hand on my knee quieted me instantly and a chill rolled up my spine. My love owned me and my voice halted at her silent command.

"I'm done wasting my breath on Warren. He doesn't get any more of my time, my thoughts, regrets or 'what ifs.' I'm sure you're worried about your sister, but he doesn't deserve your energy, Leo. I had a perfect day with you. Watching you embrace my friends as your own and seeing your face light up when Elizabeth laughed at the fish—I almost forgot that we hadn't always been together.... Don't let him ruin this day. Don't let him be any part of us. Not again."

My jaw clenched, my eyes slamming shut as pain ricocheted in my head. I opened my eyes and stared at her. The short, soft wave of her deep burgundy hair caressing her cheek begged to be touched as loudly as her full lips asked to be kissed. I wanted to obey her and force him from my mind, never giving him a second thought, but I couldn't. The guilt that catapulted me into reaching out to her one more time before attempting to let go swung through me with the strength of a tidal wave.

"But he is a part of us. He's the entire reason for us. If I hadn't pleaded with Marie to stop seeing him, he might never have found you. And if you hadn't been with him—if he hadn't hurt you—then you might never have come to Salem. He's the catalyst for all of this. Loving you has rocked my world, Sloane, but he's the fucking epicenter!"

My voice echoed in the car and my throat ached. I felt my breath leave my body and darkness leech into my vision from the periphery as I gasped for air. My hands trembled. I balled them into fists to stop the unwanted shockwave rolling through my bones. Sloane's hand on my face felt cold and her voice sounded miles away as she spoke words I couldn't decipher. I tried to see her but as I heaved another breath through my clenched teeth, my heartbeat turned violent and my face burned with heat. I was bottoming out, losing control like never before, and it was all because of him.

CHAPTER FIFTEEN

Sloane

"Leo? Leo, look at me," I demanded, trying to keep my voice as calm as possible.

He shook his head, eyes closed, fists at his temples. I'd only ever seen the glazed, faraway look in his eyes one other time. The day he called out "black" during our scene then locked himself in the bathroom. I understood now what he'd called a drop, the drowning feeling that comes from losing yourself so deep in the darkness of a scene that you can't climb out immediately, not even with the warm touch of your lover or soothing words from the one with whom you'd exchanged power. After I left him, I'd researched that element of play and guilt plagued me, wondering if he'd ever managed to come out of it.

I made my way to the driver's side door, opening it and crouching beside Leo, who remained motionless and bound in mental knots. I took his hands, pulling them from his head and rested them in his lap clasped in mine.

"Leo?"

He sighed and slowly opened his eyes just a slit, his forehead still creased with deep lines of tension.

"He's nothing but a coincidence to you and me. An unfortunate coincidence. But a meaningless one. It doesn't matter how he came into my life—why or when—because he's out of my life now. And it doesn't matter how I found you, it just matters that you were here waiting for me. What if all of this, every hard year, angry moment, and sad turn of events led us to each other to be happy?"

"How can you believe in the kind of fate that would break your heart countless times?" he asked, then his voice dropped to a whisper. "How do you know I'll even make you happy in the end? What if we're not right for each other? You don't even know how fucked up I am."

I breathed deeply, hating the melancholy in his voice. We were two of a kind, both hopelessly hopeless, worried for all our days that our darkness and damage would never let us be anything more than damaged and dark. But he was wrong. It was like Bryon told me before, just because we both had seams —held together by glue—didn't mean we were still broken. I'd found the glue too many times to count but it didn't matter so long as Leo loved me despite the cracks along my surface.

"So you're fucked up. I'm fucked up. Bryon's fucked up. Oliver's fucked up. My parents were fucked up. And some day little Elizabeth will be fucked up because everyone has shit that breaks them. Everyone has damage that changes them; that's just life and we *must* accept it and keep going. What matters is that we don't let it stop us from being happy. We can be fucked up and blissfully content at the same time, Leo."

He pulled in a breath through his nose slowly and stared into space. After a few agonizingly slow minutes, Leo shook his head almost indiscernibly then spoke, his voice low and steady. Dark.

"But that's what you don't understand. I'm not damaged. No one died, no one hit me, no one broke me down and made me this way. It'd be a whole lot easier to wrap my head around the fact that I want to hurt the woman I love if I had some sob story about how Daddy Calloway beat the shit out of me or if some crazy neighbor made me watch a snuff film when I was a kid. None of that happened. My darkness doesn't come from tragedy. It comes from my heart. It's just who I am. And that scares the shit out of me." His voice broke and his breath hitched as he choked back a flood of emotion with everything he had. "And it should scare you. Why doesn't it scare you, Sloane?"

I squeezed his hands in mine, watching his jaw shift as he continued to stave off tears. "Because I love you," I whispered.

His eyes grazed up my crouched body, from our hands to my face. He'd said it so many times since the dinner that reinstated us as friends and I'd held on to those words as tightly as I could, only offering them once. I'd never stopped loving him. I loved him before I knew this deeper side of him. Before he'd submitted to me and relinquished ultimate control of our relationship. I loved Leo in a way I'd never loved Warren. A way I'd never loved anyone. The kind of love that made me sink into his ocean, floating into the horizon with no fear of drowning or losing myself to the salty waves. Leo's waters held me safely. His arms, his rope, his leather, his love bound me as carefully as a swaddled baby—tenderly and with the utmost care.

"I love you, Leo," I reiterated. "You think your darkness is scary, but to me, it's home. It's like turning off the lights and letting the night wrap me up. In the dark of you, I relax. I give in. I don't care why you are the way you are, I just care that you choose to be that way with me. Because I need it. I crave it. I need you to be my demon, remember? Because I can't be my own anymore. I can't punish myself for the things that haunt me."

His blue gaze drifted over my cheekbones as he sighed, squeezing my hands firmly. He nodded and I began to rise to my feet as I murmured, "Take me home, Sir."

"Yes, my love," he breathed as he turned the key in the ignition.

I hadn't been inside Leo's home since the day we'd left for Oliver's house—the day it all came to a screeching halt. Leo didn't make any reference to the last time I'd been in his place as he closed the door behind us, leaving the quiet car ride and his panic back at the aquarium. He said something about changing his clothes and rushed to his bedroom while I shifted my weight from one foot to the other in the kitchen, glancing around and trying not to remember the trauma that had followed my last overnight visit.

"Sloane, can you come in here please?" Leo called from his bedroom.

My stomach fluttered with glee and I wondered what might await. I didn't speak as I let my feet guide me to the bedroom that had been a part of so much of "us." The room where he'd christened my body and my skin his with the deep red rouging along my panty line.... *Mine.* The bathroom where he'd first touched me bare and the sheets that I'd come on more times than I could count—tied, bound, and free.

I saw the light on in the bathroom connected to his bedroom and approached the half-open door. I locked eyes with the lion on Leo's back and smiled softly. That beast had come to mean so much to me. From menacing and powerful, secretive and stoic, to simply the art gracing my lover's skin—that lion looked through me the way I looked through it. Dressed in only red gym shorts slung low on his hips, showing off the tattoo and the strong muscles of his back, he turned, muscles rippling and nearly eliciting a moan from me.

I almost laughed when I looked at his face. From his throat to his nose and from ear to ear, his face was covered in thick, foamy, white shaving cream. I had to giggle. He rolled his eyes.

"Red shorts, white beard, abs...you're like sexy Santa," I chuckled.

He reached for my hand and drew me into the bathroom before grabbing my waist and propping me up on the counter in front of him.

"Well, maybe if you're a good girl Santa will give you what you want," he teased.

His fingers barely brushed the skin of my sides, slipping under my shirt as he held me still on the countertop. I watched his eyes drift to the spot near my thigh and I followed. Sitting on the white marble was a five blade, black and silver handled razor and next to that was a shiny blade that would've made Sweeney Todd jealous, unfolded and glimmering in the florescent lights.

"Take your pick," he said quietly.

"What?"

"You said you liked me better without it, so would you like to help me get rid of it?"

I glanced at the two razors at my side then back at him, my eyes growing wide. "You'd let me put that blade to your throat?"

Leo's eyes narrowed, his palms pressing into the vanity as he leaned in close to my face. "I'd let you do anything," he replied, drawing out the words slowly in a deep rasp.

"Anything?"

He scoffed with a bit of a laugh and pulled back, the white lathered foam on his jaw shifting with his bashful grin. "Okay, maybe not everything." He chuckled. "I'm not that progressive. But...blindfold me, tie me up, whip me, flog me, shave this beard from my face. Whatever you want," he said. He pointed a finger at me, potentially reading the wild ideas that had sprung up in my mind. "Within reason."

The cheeky smirk on his lips was infectious and I nodded absently, looking over my instrument choices. I didn't know how to wield a straight razor and I didn't trust myself not to mar his perfect face with my novice touch, so I grabbed the standard five-blade. It looked nicer than the one I used to shave my legs. Raising it to his cheek, he locked eyes with me.

"With the grain, short strokes."

He reached beside me to the faucet, turning on a slow, steady trickle of warm water. I placed my free hand on his chest and sighed. I could feel the subtle rumble of his heartbeat as I began just below his right sideburn.

Watching his smooth skin appear under each stroke of the razor, watching the white cream and thick dark hair disappear, made my insides flutter with joy. My Leo was returning with every inch-wide rectangle I cleared.

His breathing remained steady and his eyes trained down on my lap as I shaved his face slowly and with care. Though he'd explained how to do it, I knew he saw this relinquishment of control to be his offering of submission. He tilted his head after I rinsed the razor under the stream of water and shook it off, returning to shave from his jawbone down his neck. He moved where I wanted without me having to ask. He puffed out his cheeks, making the skin tauter and easier to swipe over. He trusted me implicitly.

His eyes may've been averting my gaze, but he was

reading me nonetheless. And while I loved knowing he was willing to be this way for me, I suddenly felt the truth slam into my soul.

I didn't want to be his Domme. I wanted what we had back. I'd fallen in love with him as much as I'd fallen in love with our roles—our dynamic.

"I don't really want this," I whispered.

Leo straightened, his eyes growing wide as they met mine. His fingers rose slowly to brush his freshly shaven skin. "You've already done more than half of my face. It's a little late to be saying that, Sloane."

I breathed a laugh and bit my bottom lip. "Not that."

He frowned and moved closer to me, waiting.

"You know how to read me. I don't believe you've lost that ability," I said. "I don't want this."

I held out the razor to him and he took it as a knowing look washed over him. He squared his shoulders and his jaw firmed without emotion.

"Thank you for letting me try," I continued. "For loving me enough. For humbling yourself for me. But we both know that's not who I am. And I'm telling you now, that's not who I want to be."

Leo's hand rose to cup my cheek. I shut my eyes as I leaned into the touch. He let his thumb sweep over the apple of my cheek. He sighed and took his hand back.

He took the razor from my hand and silently shaved the rest of his face, looking over my shoulder into the mirror without a word as he did. I watched in awe as the man I'd fallen in love with, the one who looked straight through my walls, returned to me, not only in appearance but also in spirit. He'd never stopped being dominant, but this man before me, the one with the firm stance and the brooding, blazing, blue eyes—this man was the one who'd marked me his. And I was his.

He wiped his face clean with a towel. I boldly reached out to feel the smooth jaw I'd missed, but he snatched my wrist in his grasp. He allowed me a single stroke of his cheek, my hand guided by his force, before he placed my hand in my lap.

I noticed the faint grin on his mouth when he dragged his hand along his face, looking down briefly. When his eyes rose and met mine powerfully, I shuddered.

Leo snapped his fingers and pointed toward the bedroom. I sucked my top lip into my mouth and moved in slow motion off the countertop, letting my bare feet slide to the cool tile. Leo hadn't moved, leaving me pressed against him where I stood. Still he didn't speak. I slithered past him, feeling my heartbeat surge as the sound of his commanding snap echoed in my head. I took my careful steps out of the bathroom and toward his bed and planted myself on the edge of his thick down comforter. And I waited for my master to follow.

CHAPTER SIXTEEN

Leo

I glanced in the mirror above the sink and smiled. My face was clean shaven for the first time in months and my heart was thrumming steadily. As the familiar feelings of excitement and power leeched through me, I took a breath and gathered my supplies.

Two small washcloths were under my arm, one wet with warm water and one dry, the can of shaving foam in my hand. I pocketed the shiny straight razor, pulled my shoulders back, and took a step into my bedroom where she waited with bated breath.

I locked eyes on my good girl, perched on the foot of my bed, eyes wide and expectant. With one flicking glance up and down her body, she slowly stood and shed her clothing. I wanted to smile. I wanted to scoop her in my arms and cover her with kisses, thanking her for returning us to this place, for giving me back this thing I loved, but I resisted.

She read the silent command in my eyes and climbed back up onto the bed, naked in wait.

Slinking toward her, I set the supplies on the bed beside her thigh and carefully drew in the scent of her body, clean from her morning shower and musky from her arousal—without a hint of floral perfume. It pained me to step away from her beautiful body again, but I'd waited for this moment—for this scene—and it had to be perfect. Four steps and I reached the dresser where I opened the drawer and found my black leather gloves. As I turned, tugging them tautly onto my hands, I heard her sharp intake of breath followed by a gulp. I hadn't worn them since the night I'd called out the safe word.

My gaze dragged up her body, from the deep purple lacquer on her toes to her firm calves, loving the way her kneecaps flexed as I surveyed her, goosebumps rising along her thighs as my gaze made its way to the place where they met.

When I'd first put my hands on her pussy, it had been waxed bare, but in the weeks since we'd delved back into our relationship I noticed she'd gotten out of that practice. I was happy about it as the look of prepubescence had never really done it for me. But when she'd walked out of the bathroom, intent on submitting, I knew what I wanted to do.

I watched Sloane eyeing the items I'd placed on the bed and reached out to her, causing her to look at me instead. My black leather palms pressed into her thighs as I spread them apart. She opened to me easily and with her gaze trained keenly on my face, she leaned backwards, relaxing completely on the bed.

I let my leather-covered fingers spread her sex apart and grinned at the glisten of her arousal, her breathy sighs drifting toward the ceiling. I reached for the wet washcloth, now cooler than I'd hoped for her comfort, and pressed it between her legs. Sloane squirmed and shrieked in surprise and I chuckled.

She pushed up on her elbows and glared at me, a contemptuous grin morphing her mouth. She wanted to watch.

The shaving cream grew into a little white mountain in my hand and I slathered it along the creases of her thighs and the crest of her pubic bone. Her legs trembled when she saw me pull the straight razor from my pocket and grip it in my palm. I smiled, knowing she understood my plan.

"Know your colors?"

She licked her lips, breathless, and nodded.

With that, I began. Short strokes downward through the lathered hair left the barely rounded flesh above her slit naked. I wiped the razor on the wet washcloth occasionally; each time I returned it to her skin she gasped at the chill. With care, I stroked the hair away, eventually leaving a simple landing strip.

Sloane had fallen back on the bed again, quiet save for the few sharp breaths from the cold blade returning to her flesh. My chest burned with exhilaration that she allowed this time of dominance. I wielded a true weapon, a dangerous tool, and yet she relaxed under my touch and simply breathed through her resistance. With complete trust.

I felt my head swimming, drunk with power, and I decided to take it one step further. One hand moved to splay her reddened lips apart, showing me her intricate flower, and through what lather of foam remained and her increased arousal, a smattering of trimmed hairs protected her on the inside edge. I took another small pump of shaving cream and dabbed it along the engorged flesh of her perfect pussy, feeling her fight the urge to squirm as I nearly grazed her clit.

"Hold very still," I whispered with authority.

She froze, and the quick obedience made my dick hard.

"That's a good girl," I groaned, lifting the blade to her most sensitive flesh. With the steadiest hand and the ease and grace of a sculptor, I sheared the hair from her inner lips, listening to her lose track of a frustrated noise as I did. By the time I finished carefully clearing every bit of hair from her protected lotus, her body dripped with need and her breasts heaved with desire.

With the dry cloth, I cleaned the leftover cream from her skin and wiped my gloves clear as well. Sloane didn't move. I'd ended up bent at the waist, crouching to get the best view of her pussy as I tended to it. When I straightened to look down at her still spread for me, panting wildly with her arm thrown over her eyes, my cock twitched.

Her silence, her obedience, her swift control over her movements at my command were the most precious gift and the utmost example of the kind of submission I craved from her. She didn't fear me. She didn't humor me. She revered me and the power I held just as I revered her and the power she offered. She loved me, just as I loved her.

Shedding my gym shorts, I climbed on top of her and heard her sigh blissfully. I took her wrists in my hands and pulled her arms away from her face. Sloane blinked up at me and I saw words brimming on her tongue. But she knew better.

"Speak," I allowed.

"Was I good?" she breathed.

I beamed down at her, my eyes dancing from her swollen lips to her expectant hazel stare and the flush of her cheeks. "You were perfection."

A shy smile drifted onto her face, then grew. She giggled when I held her tightly and rolled our bodies so she lay on top of me. Though I saw how she'd relaxed, she didn't move her arms once she sat up straddling me. My cock jumped feeling her wet pussy so warm and close. Sloane, still obedient, just gazed at me, waiting for a command. That alone granted me more satisfaction than she could've ever understood.

"Touch me," I said. "Put your hands on me however you want, lovely girl. Ride my cock, my face, my fingers...make me your toy and come. Come hard. Come as many times as you need. You earned it."

Her jaw hung open for a split second and then her hands moved to graze over my bare chest. Her slender fingers skated down my stomach, the muscles tensing rigidly as her ghostly touch tickled me. Sloane inched back to straddle my thighs and I watched as her eyes fell on my firm, eagerly waiting cock. I let my arms drift above my head, folding them behind my neck. Her hands playing coyly down my abs made me grin but the second she palmed my length, I shut my eyes and moaned. I reveled in this new game we played, where I controlled her level of control. Why hadn't we known this was the right way all along?

Her eyes gleamed with lust and excitement. My breath caught when she rubbed her other hand between her legs before capturing my cock with the lubed fingers she pulled from her pussy. Sighing heavily as she worked her hands around me, I cursed myself for ever keeping a secret from her, for ever doubting that I could love a submissive. And for waiting so long to take back what was mine.

As rasps began to build in my throat, she dropped her hands and moved into position, gliding her warm pussy down over me like the most perfectly fitting glove. We moaned in unison as Sloane began to ride me, filling herself to the hilt repeatedly. Her palms slammed into the mattress on either side of my head as her hips bucked and her naked body rippled with visible chills.

I lifted my gloved hands to her sides, grazing up the sensuous curve of her waist, and found myself gripping her, helping bounce her on my dick. She boldly found my hands and moved them to cup her breasts. I toyed with them eagerly, her pleasure my one and only goal. Rolling her nipples into firm points, I tugged on them hard until she cried out through a smile. Sloane's pussy gripped me tightly and as I felt her reach the pinnacle of her orgasm, my hand instinctively flew to her throat, squeezing just enough to flush her face and give her permission to stop breathing long enough to explode more powerfully than she would without the help of my palm. She shattered, bearing down on me, her walls clamping my dick and her juices soaking me gloriously. When I released her stunningly beautiful throat, she gasped and groaned through the final wave of ecstasy.

In a few quick motions, she was off me and turned around, facing my feet with her ass in the air. I sat up and grinned.

"Tell me what you want, my love," I said.

Her short burgundy hair whipped around her face as she looked over her shoulder at me. "No," she said. "You tell me what I want."

An unexpected growl snuck out of my throat and I moved to kneel behind her in a flash. Her eyes still locked on me, I saw the wicked smirk growing on her ruby lips and without a thought, I spanked her bare ass hard enough to make her flinch and squeal. She inched forward away from me and I pulled her back, slapping the same spot again with force. The sexy squeak she released, followed by a faint giggle, gripped my stolen heart and I tried like hell to keep from smiling.

"You want to be a brat. And you want to be punished for it. Well, naughty girl, grab the end of that bed and I'll gladly make both of our days."

A stealthy breath flowed out of me when I saw it. I don't know if I'd ever truly lost the ability to read her or if I'd suppressed it of my own guilt, but it was back. The little light in her eyes before she turned to face the footboard, gripping it with both fists and bracing herself, was the same light I'd seen on day one. It was consent. A silent offering of permission and trust.

My palm cracked against her ass, thrusting her forward, and I grinned. Again, the thwack of my leather glove rang out and I watched her cheek flush pink. I doled out another and then another, loving the sounds she made. Pleasure mixed with pain. A little bratty whine crossed with a sexy sigh. When I let up for a moment she glanced over her shoulder again and bit her lip, sultry bedroom eyes peering back at me.

I smoothed my hand over the skin I'd reddened as we stared at each other. She wanted another slap, I could see it. Arching her back, she pushed back a little to keep my palm connected with her ass. I shook my head. Bratty little minx, how had I never considered that this part of her existed deep inside and needed coaxing out?

I straightened and lined the head of my cock up with her entrance. Her eyes widened with anticipation and just before I sank inside of her, I spanked her three times in a row with hard, short slaps to the same spot on her right cheek. She squeezed her eyelids shut; I watched her mouth form an O when I filled her with my length. Sloane sank back onto me, still gripping the footboard, but I took control back and held her hips to fuck her relentlessly. Her head dropped, moans dripping from her lips.

When I knew she was starting to spin out—enjoying

herself so much she began to drift off into the levitating zone of pleasure—I'd crack her ass with another firing squad round of brutal spanks until she gritted her teeth and screeched.

"Bad girl, good girl, bratty girl, controlling girl—it doesn't matter, you're mine. My girl," I said, slamming into her, feeling my dick begin to pulse.

"Mmm...yes, Sir," she moaned.

I spanked her again and she gasped but I never stopped pulling her hips back to drill her with my cock. "Mine. You're always mine."

"Yes, Sir!" she grunted, coming all over the both of us with a wail.

I reached out and took a fistful of her hair, tugging her back. Leaning over to press my cheek against hers and whisper in her ear, I came. "And I am yours, my love. All yours. Thank you."

Ben glanced at his watch and I shook my head. "I'm sorry, I'm holding you up," I said.

"No, we're cool. I was just seeing how long it's been since you took a breath."

I tilted my head and sneered, though I knew his joke was warranted. Taking an exaggeratedly long, deep breath, I forced a smile and Ben chuckled.

"I'm glad you got her back, man. I'm glad to not be

pouring you into my backseat anymore and I'm glad to see you smile for once. It's a good thing."

I absently touched the side of my face, remembering Sloane's tentative strokes with the razor and the subsequent re-do job I had to do. It'd been two weeks since that moment and everything after had been utterly perfect. Easy days and nights together. Lazy fucks and intense scenes. My love abounded in everything I did alongside Sloane. From meals to making love, next to her or inside of her, I was a better man. A whole man.

"Thanks. And thanks for being there for me through the bullshit. You're good at the whole tough love thing," I replied.

Ben threw his head back and laughed as the waiter swung by quietly with our checks. Ben grabbed his and put his credit card inside the black booklet. "If you'd gotten any worse off I might've pulled out all the stops with a good beating. Maybe make you call me Master just to prove a point. But luckily you got your shit together."

Rolling my eyes, I felt my chest puff out almost instinctually. I thanked God Sloane had righted our path and helped set our roles back into balance. I wasn't a submissive. Not by nature or by choice. I would've done anything for her, including submit, but deep down I'd always known I was meant to be her Dom.

"I should get going," I said.

The waiter had returned with our bills and once we both signed, Ben stood and offered a hand. We shook and I clapped him on the back.

"Jade wants the four of us to get together soon," he said.

"Of course. Once the wedding is over, we should be free."

Ben smiled and nodded. "Call me and tell Sloane we said hey."

The shared talk of "we" gave me a small thrill, one that I didn't know I would enjoy as much as I did. I smiled all the way to my car and when I saw the time, I figured it was a good time to head to Wendy's sister's house where the bridal shower had been happening for the past three hours.

When I arrived, the cars parked along the street had thinned and since Oliver's was sitting in the driveway with his hatchback open, half-filled with gifts, I assumed it was safe to enter.

My soon-to-be sister-in-law turned around inside the foyer with a smile, my brother at her side with his arm around her, and I smiled back.

"Hey," Oliver said.

"Hey. How was the party?" I asked, leaning in to kiss Wendy's cheek. She had a glow about her and her belly had only barely begun to swell.

"It was great," Wendy said. "I think Sloane is helping my mom and sister in the kitchen."

I nodded and slipped through the light crowd that remained clogging the entryway and found my way to the kitchen. The sight of Sloane's bright smile as she helped with dishes caused my heart to thump wildly in my chest. Before our short separation I'd envisioned a future with her, but nothing compared to the fantasies I had now. Her in an ivory dress waiting for me at the end of an aisle. Sweat beading on her brow as she used her strength to bring life into the world. I thought of it all. And often.

She handed a freshly-dried casserole dish to Wendy's mother and caught my eyes. Her sigh and smile gave me a little thrill.

"Hi." I waved and she excused herself from the cleaning crew and came toward me.

The kiss she planted on my lips was sugary, like butter-cream frosting.

"We should go," she said through a forced smile.

I chuckled softly. "Okay. Is everything all right?"

Sloane patted my bicep and nodded unconvincingly. "Yeah. Yeah. Just let me get my purse and say goodbye to Wendy."

My brow dipped down and though her quick request to leave seemed odd, I considered maybe she'd just had enough socializing for the day. Or she was itching for alone time with me, a thought I admit made me relax.

When I turned to step to the front door again, I saw my sister and stopped.

"Marie. I didn't think you were driving in for this," I mused.

Her lips pursed and she seemed to avoid my eyes, pushing a hand through her hair. "Well, she's going to be my sister-in-law. I was invited."

I gulped and wondered what the day must've been like for Sloane, sitting in the same room as Marie knowing what she knew now. "Of course," I muttered. "Where's Barry?"

As if on cue, the door flung open and my nephew raced toward his mother, his brown curls flopping in his eyes as he skidded to a halt at her feet.

"I had candy and popcorn and orange soda all for me at the movies!" he cheered.

I glared at Marie then my eyes flicked to the doorway and my stomach plummeted. Warren stood mere feet away from Sloane. His cocky smirk as he looked at my sister and the son he'd never given a damn about, coupled with the defeated expression Sloane wore next to him, made my blood boil. My fists balled at my sides, veins protruding from my forearms and heat raging along my skin.

CHAPTER SEVENTEEN

Sloane

I didn't give Warren a single glance before I marched toward Leo and put a hand on his wrist above his white-knuckled fist.

"Just take me home, okay?" I whispered.

His blue eyes flared like the most dangerous flame and he turned to his sister with a stiff jaw. "Are you fucking kidding me?" he growled at her in a hush.

"Uh-oh. That's a bad word, Uncle Leo," Barry chirped from the space between the three of us.

Leo's eyelids slipped closed and he sighed. He ruffled Barry's hair, losing the menacing fists he'd made the moment he saw Warren and apologized. "Sorry, bud. Shouldn't have said that."

I glanced back at Warren and luckily, he'd softened a bit, seemingly struck by the tornado he'd caused within this family.

"Let's go home," I reiterated. "There's nothing to say or do here."

From the moment I'd walked into the party, Marie had avoided me. I didn't necessarily want to hug it out with her, compare notes, or even claw her eyes out, but I would've been content to be cordial. She, on the other hand, faked two nice exchanges with me and ignored me the rest of the time. Wendy had plenty of friends and tons of family, so it was easy to keep our mutual silence from seeming awkward to the group, but it unsettled me. Would we ever get over this? How was I supposed to share holidays with someone who treated me as if I was invisible? Most of all, the way she treated me worried me because I knew what Leo would think. I knew it would hurt him to know his sister had disregarded me.

Halfway through the shower I heard Marie share an adorable story about Barry and the first time he met the Easter Bunny, but it was the words that followed that made the hairs on the back of my neck prickle.

"He's with his father for the day. He'll be dropping him off later."

Leo hadn't said a word about Barry spending time with Warren when he'd told me his sister was dating him again. I wondered if he had left that information out, or worse, if Leo would be shocked to hear the news, too. Judging from his reaction, he had no idea.

I'd tried to get Leo out the door as quickly as possible, but it wasn't that simple. We weren't lucky enough to avoid this interaction. And maybe it was a sign...we'd have to come to terms with these kinds of dealings for years to come. We'd overcome so much already, alone and together; we could see our way through having to deal with Warren and Marie's rekindled relationship. But guilt flooded me when I considered my hand in rekindling them. I was the one who'd shamed Warren for his lack of involvement in Barry's life, after all.

My jaw stiffened and I breathed deeply. Leo and I had to stop blaming ourselves for puppeteering these unavoidable events. I was no more to blame for Warren and Marie getting back together than Leo was to blame for me meeting Warren in the first place. We weren't that important to the universe. Things just happen. They were fucked up and unfair and I wished we could wipe them all away, but we couldn't.

I breathed a sigh of relief when Leo slipped his hand in mine and squeezed.

"I'll see you later, bud," he said to Barry.

Not another word passed between Leo and his sister as we headed for the door. He offered a clipped goodbye to Oliver and Wendy and I tried to breathe when I met Warren's gaze at the door. With the hand of the man who loved me—the one who put me first and did his best to give me everything I needed, even with his faults—I faced the man who'd used me and changed the way I looked at myself.

Warren's smirk returned as we attempted to brush by him. "Hey, Leo, haven't seen you in a while. Looks like you're doing well."

Crossing the threshold, Leo muttered something I couldn't make out. We were close to freedom, nearly out of the same breathing air when Warren chimed in again.

"Fair warning, she's got a thing for guys with their name on the front door. Sloane, your dad owned his own business, right?"

Stomach acid jumped in my throat and my face grew clammy in an instant. Leo's feet stopped dead on the concrete front stoop.

"Don't," I whispered in barely a breath, not even looking at Leo. "Please don't. Barry's right there and it's Wendy's party. It's not worth it."

Leo squeezed my hand hard and took another step away from the house. Slow and steady, we held hands in silence until we reached his car at the end of the driveway.

When he let go of my fingers to open the passenger side door for me, I knew not to speak. He stood eerily still beside the car. I slipped inside and waited until he'd closed himself in the driver's seat.

The ride back to Leo's house was so quiet my ears hummed; the sound of my breathing seemed to echo in the space. I watched his hands grip the steering wheel, flexing as tightly as possible then releasing and repeating the motion again. He huffed at every red light and I swear I could hear his teeth grinding.

We walked inside his house and I finally felt at ease enough to speak.

"Leo?'

"Yeah?" his defeated whisper nearly broke my heart.

"Do you want to...take it out on me?"

I turned to face him in the living room, feeling suddenly out of place in his space and wondering if he'd say yes to my offering. I didn't know how else to help him. I couldn't imagine the way Warren made him feel, both with his words and the mere fact that he'd shown up with Barry in tow.

Leo's eyes softened, his brow furrowing. I saw his lips part and he took two quick steps toward me, grabbing my hands in his at my sides.

"No," he whispered. "I never want that. My anger should never be connected to what we have. The night before you found out about Marie and Barry—I was angry that night. I was torn up inside, knowing how badly I needed to be honest with you. Every second I spent thinking about it made me more and more angry and afraid, especially since I'd only then realized I'd fallen in love with you. Anger has no place in a scene we share. It can only cause problems. If I want to physically express my rage, I'll go to the gym. I'll buy a punching bag. I'll beat the living shit out of Warren himself—but I will never touch you in a moment of anger ever again. I never want to be cruel to you. And I would never dream of punishing you for someone else's mistakes. I love you, Sloane."

My eyes held on our shoes and I pulled in a deep breath. While I hated thinking of that night, knowing now what had been going on in his mind, it was good to remember it. It served as a warning, a reminder that we never want to be back there. We were done silencing ourselves. Sure, we could share a moment with a look alone, but that didn't mean we shouldn't talk.

"I'm sorry you had to see him," he whispered.

Our eyes met and I melted under his tender gaze. "It's okay. Honestly, the only thing I felt when I saw him was concern for you. Seeing him didn't do anything but prove to me how much I love you."

"I'm so furious with my sister."

"I know. It's just not that simple. Warren has this way of twisting everything to make his deceit seem excusable. I feel sorry for her. You should too. She doesn't need you to be angry with her, she needs you to be there—waiting for when he breaks her heart. Because he will. When he finally broke mine, I had no one because either I was too embarrassed to share the truth with them or they were so angry with me for being so stupid that I shut them out completely. She'll need you. Barry will need you. But you can't be in control of the situation."

Leo's knuckles brushed over the apple of my cheek and I leaned into the feeling. "Very wise, my lovely girl..."

I sighed. "Maybe I am now. But I wasn't always."

His head ticked to one side and his mouth began to curve softly as he stroked my cheek. "You evolved. That's something to be proud of."

I had evolved. The months on my own in Salem, living in a quiet bubble with no friends, no job, and no life had been the first step, the initial purging of my soul. Then came my attempt at writing a book; with every line I wrote, I worked to cleanse my heart of Warren and the muck he'd left in me. Eventually Leo had held my hand with soft leather gloves and pulled me over some invisible line of reckoning. I could've gotten to this place on my own. I could've learned to release Warren from my mind and burn the remnants of our destruction if I'd never met Leo, but it might've taken longer. I might never have known this other facet of myself and the way a true, powerful partner could make me feel. Leo hadn't rescued me—I limped away on my own—but he saw me. He saw the cracks, he saw the broken bits, the bruises on my mind and the walls I'd built around myself and by some kind of miracle he looked through them and saw me at my most basic and raw form...and he loved me.

When I looked into his blue eyes and saw the barely noticeable hint of gloss coating them, I considered how Leo had changed since the first moment I met him and smiled.

"We've both evolved," I said.

I watched Barry fidgeting in his suit while Leo's hands remained firm on his shoulders, keeping him from running. His chocolate brown curls had been trimmed and sprang up into a perfectly adorable style, framing his sweet face and dark eyes. My heart rested easy. I could look at him now and not think of Warren. I no longer saw something I'd lost, I saw something that awaited me. I let my gaze drift up to his uncle, my love—my Sir—and when I caught him staring back at me with lust in his eyes, I listened to the words I knew we'd one day hear.

"I now pronounce you husband and wife."

Every guest clapped and cheered as Wendy wiped tears from under her eyes with a delicate pink handkerchief and Oliver squeezed her to his side to kiss her cheek before they descended the aisle. Wendy's sister and Leo linked arms and followed as Leo kept Barry's tiny hand in his. I shot two thumbs up at Barry and he beamed at me.

I waited in the receiving line to hug Wendy and Oliver, my eyes wetting with tears when I finally approached them.

"I'm so happy for you two," I whispered to Wendy.

Her eyes welled up then she scoffed and laughed. "I'm too hormonal for this day!" she joked.

I squeezed Oliver tightly, his smile lighting the space around them. "Congratulations."

"Thanks, Sloane," he replied.

Leo stood beside his brother, a grin painted on the mouth I longed to kiss. Ever since the night we'd washed Warren out of our minds and out of our relationship, we'd been glued to one another. If he wasn't inside me, he was touching me; if he wasn't touching me, he was whispering in my ear; and if he wasn't near me, I ached for him. Old barriers had been broken and new bonds had formed. No topic was off limits and no conversation was left unspoken. I never knew a man could be so open and honest.

"I have a surprise for you," Leo whispered, leaning into my ear, not-so-covertly grabbing a handful of my ass.

"I think it's customary to give the bride and groom a gift, not your girlfriend."

Leo growled in approval of the word and I smiled, loving every moment I elicited a reaction from him. His hot breath tickling my neck nearly had me melting right then and there, but as his family continued to file through to congratulate the newlyweds, I held back the urge.

"It's in your car. I want you wearing them at the reception."

Without knowing what he could be referring to, I felt my body grow hot. I bit my bottom lip and lowered my eyes. I let a whisper be my reply, "Yes, Sir."

My desire told me to run to the car and scramble for whatever salacious package he'd left as my surprise, but I walked briskly instead, letting my head swim with anticipation.

Sitting on the passenger seat of my car was a black box. No ribbon, no frills. Just a simple black box. My teeth captured my gloss-coated lip again, this time with more force as a beaming smile took me over. A matching set of shiny metal nipple clamps sat atop lacy black panties —crotchless.

The quick drive to the reception hall a few miles away exhilarated me as I wondered what else he might have in store for me. I hurried inside, one of the first guests to arrive. The wedding party stopped in the park to take more photos so other guests were surely taking their time. I found the ladies room and took my box of surprises in the stall with me to change. Shedding my red satin panties, I replaced them with the lacy black lingerie and shifted as my red dress fell to cover me once more. The breeze between my legs felt different and I made a mental note not to let Leo thrill me too much while sitting down so as not to leave a spot on my dress.

A deep breath filled my lungs and I shrugged my arms out of the slinky dress and pushed it to my waist. I pulled the cups of my now-mismatched red bra down and secured the first clamp with a hiss. I remembered the first time Leo used them on me. Though they were a different pair, more like large bobby pins that squeezed my nipples in a vice than the bear trap-like clip I'd just placed on myself, I recalled what he'd whispered to me.

"Second one hurts worse than the first."

I steadied myself with another shaky inhale and cursed as the little teeth sank in. "Fuck."

The pain burned in a flash the moment I relaxed my arms and with every movement after. I re-situated my bra, slinked back into the bodice of my dress, and finally the pain dulled and became tolerable.

As I washed my hands, I took in the sight of my pinked cheeks, the blush that Leo could bring out on my skin even from miles away. Straightening my dress, I felt the pinch of the clamps again and prepared to enter the reception hall, praying no member of Leo's family would hug me.

Music blared from the banquet room and the front doors opened, the rush of the bridal party poured inside with chatter and laughter. I watched as the crew headed into the reception with smiling faces, followed by the bride and groom. Eventually my eyes fell on Leo. As though he could sense me, he turned his head and grinned. When he dragged his gaze up and down my body, I shuddered, feeling the new pieces of my hidden wardrobe claim my body as much as Leo's look. With his smoldering gaze, he extended a hand toward me and I reached for him, letting him lead me to the party, our little secret hidden beneath my dress.

His warm hand smoothed over the fabric of my dress as he held my waist, swaying me to the soft music. I'd endured an hour with the clamps on so far, sitting through dinner and dancing to three songs in a row. Leo leaned in close, his lips tickling the little bit of waved hair near my cheek.

"When the song ends, kiss me on the cheek and walk toward the ladies' lounge at the back of the building. Lock the door then wait for me. I'll knock three times."

I pulled back and stared at him, wide-eyed. "Did you case this place for a hookup room?"

The smirk that tugged at his full lips made me snicker and shake my head. The song ended and he stared me down, commanding me to obey his instructions with nothing more than a look. With my shoulders rolled back, I breathed in deeply as I pushed up on my toes a bit and planted a kiss on his smooth cheek. My fingertips brushed his forearm and then I turned from him, walking away with purpose, my breasts aching heavily for release.

Only a minute or two passed between my locking the door to the empty lounge and Leo's triple knock. I turned the lock and opened the door. Leo walked in in silence and my breath caught when I saw his hands, now sheathed in black leather, lock the door behind him.

CHAPTER EIGHTEEN

Leo

My gaze moved slowly up and down Sloane's body. Her red dress had been tempting me all day. The way her breasts teased at the sweetheart neckline and her smooth legs looked capped off by black heels kept me throbbing as I walked in the private lounge I'd scouted during the venue walkthrough I'd done with Wendy and Oliver a few weeks ago.

Sloane's eyes were trained on the floor and my smile grew as I stepped closer to her. My hand rose to slip below her ear, my palm pressing against her throat where her pulse quickened. Her breath caught. We'd done this countless times, yet we still reacted to one another as though it were that first encounter on the second floor of the bookstore.

I leaned in, speaking quietly against her waved, merlot

colored hair. "Good evening, lovely girl. Are you ready to do as you're told?"

Her pink tongue flicked out against her bottom lip, covering the slightest of smiles that formed. "Always, Sir."

I turned her body around, my hands on her waist, and stepped to press my front to her back. My dick was already hard and the tiny gasp she let out when our bodies met told me she felt it too. Holding her hips, I moved forward, making her walk without a verbal command. A few steps and we were facing the full-length mirror in the corner of the room. Our eyes locked in the glass for a moment, but Sloane looked down once she caught my gaze. My palms skimmed up her sides, finding their way to her breasts. I knew she'd been a good girl and put on the nipple clamps I'd left her, as well as the crotchless panties. I felt her sudden intake of breath when I pressed my hands against the full mounds of her breasts through her dress and bra. Her eyes squinted shut and her face distorted into a wince as I let my fingers splay, then grab the way you test a fruit for its ripeness. Sloane was certainly ripe.

I dipped my face into the crook of her neck, planting a warm kiss on her ivory skin as I dragged down the zipper of her dress. The fabric slipped from her delicate shoulders to her waist and I helped it fall to the floor. I shed her bra and felt my dick jump at the sight of the nipple clamps torturing her. With each breath she drew, the metal clamps heaved; I knew the weight had to be causing her the most pleasurable pain.

As though she could hear my thoughts and the plan for

my next move, her breathing quickened. I let one black-gloved hand slide up her bare spine and push her forward.

"Put your palms on the mirror," I commanded.

She obeyed. God, she always obeyed, and it ruined me. Lowering my lips to her shoulder blade, I pressed the first of many kisses on her skin and worked my way down. I never let go of her body as my mouth traveled the length of her. When I reached her panty-clad ass, I spanked each side, one after the other. Not enough to make her cry out but enough to make her jump.

"Do you know how badly I want your ass?"

Sloane gulped and a little squeak followed. We hadn't talked about it in a while, but she knew I wanted it and I knew she'd give me what I wanted because she was a curious little minx.

I straightened and towered over her, locking eyes with her in the mirror. My hands found their way between her legs to the place where fabric didn't exist. I sighed at her quiet moan.

Rubbing my leather covered fingers against her clit worked her breathing to a steady pant. I spread the evidence of her arousal to her ass, feeling her shudder as I lubed her up with her own slickness. Was it the nipple clamps, the crotchless panties, the thought of me claiming her ass, or simply us finding our way back into this groove that made her so wet? For good measure, I pulled the tiny bottle of lube I'd brought with me in anticipation of this encounter from the pocket of my pants and smeared her tight asshole again, letting one finger dip inside as she gasped. I knew Sloane loved the feeling of leather inside her, but her deep moan as I carefully added a second finger assured me she was more eager for my dick. I undid my pants and let them drop to my shins then lubed myself from the small bottle, sighing at how rock hard I'd become.

Leaning over her shoulder, I captured Sloane's earlobe between my lips and growled as I let my tongue sweep over the soft skin. My breath heated her flesh as I gripped her hips and angled her so she could feel me pressing against the new part of her I was about to fuck. I started to push into her as gently as I could manage, though the urge to go deep rippled through me. My hands held her waist firmly, pulling her back at the same time I thrust forward. Her head dropped a little and I heard a noise I'd never heard from her before. It was somewhere between pain and pleasure. The sound was an auditory aphrodisiac only made better by the goosebumps I saw rising on her back and arms.

I pushed a little deeper, nearly settling inside her completely when I felt her reach back with one hand to grip my thigh.

"Yellow," she breathed.

My grasp on her hips instantly softened. "Are you okay?"

Sloane nodded and we locked eyes in the mirror. Her flushed cheeks and full, parted lips eased the bit of panic that had lit through me at the utterance of one of our safe words. She smiled a little, her eyes darting around briefly.

"Yeah," she said.

"I have more lube. Am I hurting you?"

Sloane swallowed and shook her head. "Surprisingly, no," she said. Her eyes closed and she wet her engorged lips after a soft pant. "It's actually starting to feel good."

Fuck. My hands instinctively resumed their rough hold on her body and my dick twitched inside her. She let out a breath of a moan and I bent to press my lips to the curve of her neck. "Why yellow then?"

"Just go slow. Okay?"

I snaked one hand up her spine and threaded my fingers into the short deep red strands of her hair. "Of course, my love," I whispered against her ear before inching the rest of the way into her ass.

My first slow thrust evoked a gasp from her and I stopped, waiting to hear another color, but only heard a moan follow. I moved in her once more, slowly as she'd wished. I felt the tension in her limbs loosen and I took the cue to keep going. Every push drew another lovely noise from her throat. She was sinking back on to me as I pumped into her and I knew whatever pain she'd been anticipating when she'd said yellow had never manifested in her body. I reached around and toyed with the metal clamps on her nipples, my fingers plucking the torture devices devilishly. Sloane gasped and her knees buckled. She dropped lower, smashing her forearms and cheek against the glass in front of her. I grinned and continued to tweak her breasts while I watched her lipstick smear where her breath fogged up the mirror.

Every move I made, fucking her ass a little harder with each passing second, built a chorus of guttural noises in her lungs. Sloane pushed back, lifting her face off the mirror but kept her forearms in place for stability. I caught her gaze in the mirror and saw her eyes darken with lust. Something shifted inside me as I watched her succumb to her primal desires—rocking backwards a little faster to facilitate me fucking her tight little ass. As her body clenched around my length and fire burned deep in her eyes, I wanted desperately to know how wet she was. I needed to feel her.

Holding on to her waist with one hand, my other hand rose to my mouth and I bit the leather fingertips one by one until the glove slipped loose. With my teeth clamped on the middle finger of the black glove I yanked it off and saw Sloane's expression change in the mirror. I grinned at her and let my bare hand slip between her legs.

A deep groan passed my lips and my head fell forward to rest against her back. "Oh, you dirty girl," I puffed. "I'd say you're enjoying this a little too much."

With that, I thrust into her ass relentlessly and saw the same pleasurable pain cross her face. My hand rubbed over her clit, taking cues from the noises she exhaled until we both reached the edge of the cliff. Her thighs involuntarily closed, trapping my bare hand as one last pump resulted in my undoing.

"Fuck," I breathed, dropping my head against her shoulder. My other arm held her around her waist as I felt her body shudder. Her legs trembled as a quiet whimper, something like an innocent coo, passed her lips.

I wasn't sure I'd ever known a stronger feeling of satisfaction than the one that came with the power to evoke such an array of delightful noises from my lover. We separated slowly and she turned to kiss me. The softness of her lips, swollen from arousal, helped my breathing return to normal. She bit her bottom lip, looking up at me with a silly, satisfied grin, and excused herself to the restroom.

I hated to rinse her scent away, but we had a wedding reception to finish. Washing my hands and straightening my suit, I smiled. We were back to that place, the perfect zone where I read her thoughts and desires and she heard my silently offered commands, eager to obey them. And yet, it was different than before. I saw more in her eyes than submission and devotion. I saw love and commitment, the same fire that I knew lit my eyes when I looked at her and knew we were closer than before. We were more powerful together than we ever could be alone. It was the kind of power than almost frightened me and yet I knew it was all I'd ever been searching for. A woman to laugh with, to live with, to lay beside and to hover above. Suddenly, and in slow motion, she became my world. And for one perfect moment as I looked in the mirror at the gleam in my formerly darkened eyes and my kiss-flushed smiling lips, I didn't have a single doubt.

The party was in full swing, lights flashing and music thumping as nearly every guest covered the dance floor. I headed to our table and sipped the glass of red wine I'd ordered before our impromptu scene. Sloane's Pinot Grigio sat untouched alongside her sparkly clutch purse, her phone sitting on top of it.

My head rose when I heard the familiar laughter of my nephew. I beamed the moment I saw Sloane spinning him around on the dance floor, his wild brown curls bouncing as they twirled.

The look on Sloane's face was exuberant. She'd completely let go of whatever feelings had surfaced once that devastating blow of my omission had hit her. For once I believed it, that she could love Barry despite his father, despite the circumstances of how she'd found out.

I grabbed Sloane's phone and headed to the edge of the dance floor where I began to snap photos of her and Barry twirling and laughing and wiggling their limbs. I couldn't hear anything more than her chuckles over the music, but I saw Barry motioning to her as though he was offering up new dance moves for her to try. My parents stood not far from them on the floor. They were watching too. With love in their eyes.

I sighed and smiled, walking back to the table to finish my wine. My thumb swiped over her screen, reviewing the photos I'd managed to get. One perfectly blurred image captured the moment as I'd branded it in my mind. I continued to thumb through the photos until I halted on an image of a dick that wasn't mine.

Sloane had never been squeamish about porn, but this didn't look like something saved from one of her secret sites. Something about this looked real. My heart hardened in my chest as my blood began to race and though I tried to fight it with everything inside me, I let my thumb drag across the screen to reveal the next photo. My eyelashes twitched, a fluttering pulse of anxiety that had to release somewhere as I saw a different angle of the same man—the tattoos on his arms lining up in my mind. My stomach flipped and started a slow descent, falling from what felt like my throat to my ankles as I advanced to the next photo and saw Ethan's dumb fucking face grinning at me like an idiot. Shirtless. Sweaty. Disheveled. Hard.

The tendons in my hands and arms flexed almost painfully and I flicked my thumb over the glass again.

There on the screen was the confirmation I'd been dreading. The whisper of a smile on Sloane's face as her arms lay gently over her head, rested back on plush pillows, her breasts bare...

"I thought I was exhausted before," Sloane huffed from behind me. Her arms encircled my waist and I froze. "You Calloway boys are set on wearing me out one way or another."

She moved to look up at me and I sat the phone down.

"What's the matter?"

I didn't let my eyes land on her. Staring at nothingness, darkness encroached on my vision from the periphery. I pressed my mouth in a firm line.

"Ethan."

I could hear her gulp. Her hands fell from my body and she moved to butt herself against the banquet table, set to perfection with nothing but drinks and cake crumbs left among the décor.

I saw her eyes flick downward and heard a sharp intake of her breath.

"You were going through my phone?"

"I was taking pictures of you dancing with Barry...I started to look back through them." My voice faded into the swarming sound of polka music as "The Chicken Dance" began to blare. I shut my eyes and balled my fists. I didn't want to hear the goddamn "Chicken Dance" and I certainly didn't want Barry running up to break into this exchange. My feet led me without another thought and though I felt her reach for my forearm and call my name, I kept walking.

Past one set of doors and then another, my face burned the moment fresh air touched my skin and filled my lungs. I figured I'd want to scream, but I had no words. It would've been like me to hit something, but I had no strength.

"Leo, wait!"

Sloane's voice did that thing to my body that it had always done. The hairs on my neck stood up as a satisfying chill flashed through me and my stomach clenched tight, waiting for more. Only the feeling felt stuck. The familiar chill stuttered through the thickness of my flesh and my stomach closed in on itself so tightly I thought I might be sick.

"Please let me explain," she choked.

She didn't need to explain; I saw the date on the photos. As horrible as it felt to look at those pictures and understand what they meant, I deserved that pain for what I'd done to her—for what I'd done to us.

Still, the rational thoughts didn't outweigh my anger.

Anger at the thought of another man touching her, kissing her, fucking her. Anger at myself for having driven the wedge between us that led her into another man's arms. Anger at my sister for her role in all this and anger at Warren for his masterful manipulation of both Marie and Sloane.

I blinked and saw red as waves of emotion battered me from the inside. Moments and memories hurdled through my mind faster than I could keep up with. Things I'd never given a second thought to suddenly triggered rage and as I felt Sloane's hand rest gently on my shoulder blade, I succumbed to the fire that had kindled in my soul. My mind blazed as I spun to see her fearful stare.

A stammering breath passed my lips.

"Leo—" she whispered.

My eyes traced every curve of her face and for a moment a breeze blew out the fire and ash settled like snowflakes as my temper snuffed out. I didn't need to hear an apology. She had nothing to be sorry for. A few more breaths and I'd be fine. Just a couple seconds and I'd shake this dark hand gripping me too tightly.

Sloane turned her head at the sound of jingling car keys not far away and I watched her face fall.

The moment blurred as I followed her gaze, hearing her beg me not to look. Her voice echoing in my head as I set my eyes on Marie and Warren embracing, his lips crushed against hers and his hand gripping her ass.

Red.

Another foggy moment painted crimson, the sound of

my heartbeat drumming in my ears, and in a split second I was within reach of him.

I threw the first punch, knocking him across the jaw. His eyes flared and he steadied himself, throwing one back at me. I felt my face throb and my teeth screech as I clenched down, caught by surprise that he'd hit me back so quickly. The pain didn't stop me though. Nothing would stop me. I swung again and he ducked but my feet pushed me forward and eventually I was close enough to make contact again. He came for me once more, clipping my chin and lighting another shock of pain through my jaw. I tasted blood and when I saw that asshole grin as he shuffled toward me, his fists up and at the ready, a new darkness bloomed within me. I lunged for him.

Marie screamed.

Sloane screamed.

Warren's body made a thud as he hit the ground and I scrambled to hover over him. I felt hands tugging at my clothes, my shoulders, even my neck, but my fists followed the animal instinct within me. Voices begged me to stop. I felt more pairs of eyes on me, but each punch led to the next. I succumbed to the rage I'd felt so many times over the years thinking of this man and the pain he caused. The rhythmic action of my fist hitting the hard bones of his face felt good. I couldn't stop. Anger possessed me and moved through my limbs, beating the hell out of the man I wished dead.

A force threw me backwards. My head smacked the pavement and more cries rang through the night air. I blinked up at the stars and the fog cleared. The frantic voices grew louder. I heard my sister crying, my father cursing—the one voice I didn't hear was Sloane's. I gulped and sat up, looking for her. When I found her I followed her stunned gaze yet again to see what I'd done.

Warren lay bloodied on the pavement and for a split second my gut trembled at the eerie stillness of his body. He groaned and Marie and my father helped him sit up, holding a towel to his face that immediately stained bright red.

I glanced down at my hands covered in the same shade, my knuckles nicked, throbbing, and trembling.

My eyes lifted to see Sloane one more time as sirens blared, her beautiful face bathed in flashing red and blue light.

The paramedics poured of out the ambulance, immediately asking questions and speaking code to one another as they helped Warren onto a stretcher. I felt firm hands touch my shoulders and turn me around. I heard my father say something about a lawyer and before I knew it I was in handcuffs.

Sloane's gaze grew watery as the officer read me my rights and put a hand on my head, guiding me into the back of the squad car.

"I'm sorry," I mouthed.

Sloane shut her eyes and tears trailed down her cheeks.

CHAPTER NINETEEN

Sloane

Bryon's jaw shifted as though he wanted to say something. How could he not? I'd waited three weeks to tell him about what happened at Wendy and Oliver's wedding and when the bombshell finally dropped—Leo's arrest—his eyes had nearly popped from his skull.

"Warren isn't pressing charges," I added, to which Bryon exhaled heavily and nodded with a slow blink. I was just as thankful for that fact. "Most likely because he didn't want to have to explain it to his wife. Not sure how he explained the broken nose, but that's not my business."

"How's Leo after all this?"

I gulped. "We haven't talked."

"What?" Bryon asked incredulously. "You cannot keep doing this, Sloane."

I jerked my chin down and glared at him. "Excuse me?"

Bryon's hands grew animated, waving wildly in the air,

some nerve struck deep within him. "You can't keep avoiding every fucking problem. Talk to your boyfriend. He needs you. You need him. You don't even know how he's doing after being arrested? After all you went through to get back together you don't even speak to him?"

I swallowed the lump that had grown in my throat as he berated me. My teeth nipped at my bottom lip and I evaded his stare. "I'm not avoiding him," I whispered. "He won't return my calls."

Bryon made a quiet noise then let out a sigh. "Oh. Shit. I'm...sorry."

I'd spent the past three weeks calling and texting Leo with no success. I'd stopped by the store a few times, but he hadn't been there. The only thing I hadn't tried was showing up at his door. I didn't know what was holding me back. I couldn't help but feel responsible for what sent him into such a crazed state. If he'd never seen those photos on my phone he might not have lost control when he saw Warren and Marie.

The responsibility I felt watching as he pummeled Warren still ate away at my nerves even three weeks later. Warren deserved to get his ass kicked. My God, I'd wished the man dead on multiple occasions. But Leo didn't deserve to feel that level of anger. He didn't deserve to find himself in a hole so dark that all he could do was lash out violently. I did that. I did that by being yet another woman in Leo's life who'd once upon a time fallen for Warren's bullshit. And I did that by foolishly hooking up with Ethan to try to ease my own pain when Leo and I were apart.

Bryon must've seen the tears welling in my eyes because he mercifully changed the subject, launching into a story about the annoying coworker he vented about often. I did my best to listen and not drift into the corners of my mind.

I'd been staring at my keys on the coffee table for close to an hour. The skin of my bottom lip had been chewed raw as I contemplated what to do. Our entire history—from the spilled coffee on a leather bound copy of *The Scarlet Letter* to the spilled blood of my ex-lover on what was supposed to be a happy day for Leo's family—ricocheted through my mind, bringing up the darkest of memories along with the highest of highs.

I grabbed my keys and let my heart take over, driving straight to Leo's house. I didn't let myself sit in the car and ponder any longer. Marching up to his front door, I banged on the solid wood until I heard him curse behind it.

"Jesus Christ, okay!" Leo barked as he swung open the door.

My fist still raised in the air, I stood stunned for a brief moment, locking eyes with him. His brow lifted at the sight of me and then I watched his expression crumble and his gaze fall to the ground.

"Can I come in?" I asked.

He raked a hand through his hair as he mulled over my seemingly simple question. He eventually nodded and stepped aside to allow me in. I walked in and let more memories flood my senses, causing my insides to ache for better times and for his touch—gentle or commanding. We stood in the entryway, tension thickening between us for minutes that felt eternal. He finally spoke.

"Why are you here?"

Blinking in disbelief, I shot him a hard look. He read my thoughts, pressed his lips together, and dodged my eyes again.

Suddenly, fire lit through me and I felt what he must have felt so many times—the urge to fight. Not to fight with him but *for* him. For us. Squaring my shoulders, I took a step closer to him to breathe in the scent of his body.

"Leo, there's a lot I don't know. I don't know why I was ever with Warren. Or Ethan, for that matter. I don't know where my next dollar is coming from. I don't really know how to make new friends and you already know I don't know how to date. Some days I don't know how to function without my parents. And some days I don't know if my life would be any different if they'd never died. I don't know what my future holds. But I know—goddammit, Leo—I *know* it has to include you."

I took a breath and steadied my shaking hands, noticing how Leo's expression had softened and his eyes had grown expectant.

"You woke me up. You...you made my life a fucking carousel." I choked on the sob that had caught me by surprise. "I belong to you, Leo. I belong to you."

Leo grabbed me by the shoulders and kissed me hard as tears slipped down my cheeks. His soft lips crushing against mine spread warmth throughout my body. The feeling of his strong, bare hands on me melted the chill that had begun to settle in my soul during our time apart. I sank into his chest as he wrapped his arms around me tightly.

After we breathed in sync for a few moments, he pulled back from me to look in my eyes. I couldn't tell if he wanted to speak or if he simply needed to hold my gaze. His tongue wet his lips.

"I'm sorry," I said. "I know you probably didn't want to see me after the pictures...I just—"

"What?" Leo breathed, his hand trailing down my spine then drawing me nearer to him once more with the weight of his palm. He rested his cheek on the top of my head and stroked my back tenderly. "Sloane, I don't care about that at all."

"I just feel like I'm the reason you...did what you did to Warren."

He inhaled sharply and moved to meet my eyes again. His blue stare pinned me firmly as he carefully formed his words. "You are not to blame for any of what happened that night," he said. "I invaded your privacy. I overreacted. I lost control. I'm at fault for all of it, Sloane. I'm so ashamed that you had to see me in my darkest moment."

Reaching out, I stroked the smooth side of his jaw with my fingertips then rested my palm against his cheek. I watched in shock as Leo shut his eyes and leaned into my touch. Regret crushed me that I hadn't shown up sooner to be with him. He'd been dealing with what he'd done alone, and it was clear to see he hadn't been coping well.

"This ends now," I said clearly.

Leo's eyes flashed open and he cocked his head. "Excuse me?"

My former glimmer of dominance flared and my shoulders straightened. "Do you love me?"

"Yes, of course," he said. "Don't ever doubt—"

"I'm talking."

Leo's brow jumped for a moment then his eyes narrowed on me.

"You've had three weeks to talk to me and you didn't. So now, you listen."

My gut trembled a little as the role I'd once claimed and then given up possessed me. Leo's gaze softened and though I saw tension in his jaw, he nodded slightly, waiting for me to go on.

"You love me, but are you actually in this with me?"

Lines broke across his forehead as he spoke. "Forever."

"Then this bullshit ends," I said. "Forever isn't a guarantee. We aren't doing each other any good by shutting down when things get difficult. You aren't protecting me by avoiding me. No more secrets, no more deciding what's best for me without asking me. And I won't do that to you either." I drew in a deep breath and prepared to tell the truth. "I slept with Ethan while we were broken up."

His jaw tightened even more but to my surprise he remained silent.

"It was my futile attempt at getting over you and all it did was make me miss you. I'm not proud of what I did mostly because I used him. I treated him like a plaything instead of a person and I didn't like it. I wasn't myself without you, Leo. Not then and not these last few weeks."

Leo's eyes fixed on the floor. "I'm not myself without you either."

I reached for his hand at his side.

"I'm a better man with you, Sloane."

A sigh rushed from my lungs. I was a better person with him at my side. With his power over me, I grew more powerful. With his care for me, I cared more for myself. With his passion, I flourished.

"Then we agree to move forward as one. Nothing left standing between us. Okay?"

Leo took my face in his hands. I melted under his touch, shutting my eyes and praying he'd understand my need for resolution.

He didn't speak. With sincerity in his gaze and the most earnest expression I'd ever seen, his head trembled in a nod. His lips touched mine and I moaned into his mouth. I felt his arms encircle my waist and the dominance I'd asserted just minutes before to show Leo how serious I was dissolved. I became myself once more under his hands. Leo's strong arms lifted me off the ground and I clung to him as he walked me into his bedroom.

It wasn't until he'd carefully and completely undressed both of us that I noticed the absence of his black leather gloves. He didn't move for where he normally stored them in the nightstand. As I held my breath, waiting for the energy to change, he must have noticed. Leo smoothed his bare hands over my cheeks, then my hair as I slowly lay back against the bed pillows.

"Not tonight," he whispered. "Nothing between us."

I heard myself swallow. The tone in his voice reminded me of the moment he asked if he could kiss me while we sat on a blanket under the stars. He'd always had a tender side, a loving touch underneath his dominance. There had always been a part of him that was susceptible to raw moments like this one.

Reaching out to stroke his jaw, I reveled in the newness of him all over again. I used to think he was Jekyll and Hyde, changing on a dime and never letting me in. But I was wrong. Leo was complicated, layered, much like everyone else—like me. Over time his layers had been pulled back to reveal the man I truly loved. Strong and dominant, powerful and commanding yet sweet and caring, deeply romantic and loyal to a fault.

Leo the lionhearted. King of my body and soul.

His gentle hands swept from my jaw to my breasts, his thumbs tracing the taut peaks of my nipples. Leo's mouth claimed one rosy pebble, evoking a whimper from my throat as his tongue swirled around. I let my hands thread through his raven hair and heard him sigh at the feeling. My freedom to touch him, his bare hands claiming me—it was unlike any encounter we'd ever had.

Intoxicated by the moment, every touch left a vibration in its wake. My senses documented the memory. The color of his eyes illuminated in a new light, the scent of his sweat mixing with mine, the sound of his fingers dipping inside of me, the taste of his tongue in my mouth, the feel of our bodies connecting and moving as one.

I clung to Leo as he rocked in and out of me gently. Fire built in my spine and chills scattered across my flesh as I felt impending release. The sound of his breath echoed in my mind. His fingertips pressed into my shoulders and that slight bit of roughness pushed me over the edge. My legs wrapped around his hips, trembling as ecstasy rocked my entire body. Leo pushed my hair back from my face as I continued to free float, lost in the spin of my orgasm. He thrust a few more times before reaching his own pinnacle. His lips crushed against mine as he came.

Our panting breaths slowed in time with one another, soft kisses exchanged as our bodies relaxed from shoulders to toes. Leo rolled off me but didn't leave my side, holding me close while we both came back to Earth. My eyes fluttered closed, the rise and fall of his chest against my ear lulling me to sleep. I felt the deep rumble of his voice and heard the words I'd missed just as I drifted off.

"I love you, Sloane."

CHAPTER TWENTY

Leo

Sloane's fingers gently stroked my chest and I woke from the quick sleep I'd fallen into beside her. I tucked my chin so I could kiss her hairline. I couldn't think of a time I'd allowed myself to be so vulnerable. Even when I'd once submitted to Sloane in attempt to win her back and prove my love for her I hadn't felt as raw and exposed—as truly open as I'd just been while making love to her.

I'd never felt closer to another person in my entire life and I was so grateful I'd experienced that with her. I felt her shift at my side, the stickiness of our dried sweat making our skin kiss.

She sighed. "I'm hungry."

I let out a chuckle and gently slid my arm out from under her. "I'll go get us something. Do you want some water?"

"Mmm hmm," she hummed with a sleepy grin as her

arms stretched above her head. Sloane nuzzled her face into her pillow, her hands drifting back down across her naked body as I found my boxers.

In the kitchen I sliced up some cheese and threw some crackers and grapes on a plate then filled up my two largest glasses with ice and water. I could've gone for a burger, quite honestly, but didn't have it in me to get dressed and run out. I balanced the plate and two glasses as I headed back into my bedroom where Sloane had dozed off again. When the weight of my body jostled the mattress, she hummed again and her eyes fluttered open. She'd barely caught sight of the snacks I'd brought when her hand darted out to take some cheese.

A grin formed on her lips as she ate three pieces and two crackers, barely pausing between each bite. She took a few gulps of water and laughed when she saw my wide-eyed look, watching her inhale nearly half the plate of food I'd made.

"Sorry," she said.

I smiled. "Don't be."

She took another drink then her eyes told me she had something to say. I'd missed reading her. I ate a cracker and waited for her to speak.

"What happened that night after they took you away?"

Her voice was quiet as she asked the question I'd been expecting. Shame rolled through me remembering my despicable violence and subsequent arrest. But I owed her the truth.

"You know, it wasn't exactly like in the movies. It was

less scary and more embarrassing. There was paperwork, they fingerprinted me, I had my own private photoshoot..." I grimaced, trying to make light of the worst night of my life.

Sloane reached for my hand and squeezed my fingers.

"Nothing will cut a Dom down to size faster than a strip search and seven hours sitting in a cell that smells like vomit, listening to one man cry and two others hash out who's the greatest female porn actress of all time."

"Who did you call?" she asked.

"My dad."

She breathed a heavy sigh and shook her head, her eyes still wrought with pity. "God, it felt like the cops got there immediately. Who even called the police?"

I shut my eyes and tried to will away my lingering anger as I answered. "My mother."

Sloane gaped at me. "What?"

"A guest told her there was a fight outside and she wasn't going to have her son's day ruined by some drunken idiot. She didn't know it was me. They had to have been right around the corner. Did they question you?"

She nodded but I didn't ask more. It didn't matter.

"I had to pay a fine and my dad brought a lawyer, so I have to pay him." I raked a hand through my hair and set my eyes on my love once more. "But I got lucky. I'm lucky Warren didn't press charges and I'm lucky the state didn't pursue it...this was a free one and a wakeup call that I need to get my anger in check. There's this support group therapy thing on Sundays..."

Sloane's brow rose. "Wow," she said on a breath. "That's great. Is it...helping you?"

"I think so," I replied. "I've never looked at myself as someone who has unresolved baggage, but I think I was wrong. It's hard to admit you're not perfect. It's hard to admit that you're not even okay."

She reached out for another cracker and offered a sad smile. "It's hard to admit you can't always be in control..."

I blinked and nodded, knowing how wise my love was in saying that. I reached out and smoothed my fingers over the apple of her cheek. "All of it is harder when you're alone."

Sloane leaned in, my hand trailing to the back of her neck as she spoke against my mouth. "Good thing you don't have to worry about that anymore."

She pressed her lips to mine and as I gripped her short hair gently, I coaxed a deeper kiss from her. We melted together once more, tongues and limbs dancing as raw passion and overwhelming love consumed us both. No one in control, no orders given or obeyed, and the imperfections quiet while we worshiped one another for exactly who we were.

***

"Mmm. Oh, hell yes," I groaned.

Sloane laughed and handed me a napkin. "Dear God," she said. "You're making a mess. Are you trying to live inside that burger?"

I swallowed that first delicious bite of medium-well beef and wiped my chin with a smirk. "Would that I could, my love."

She snickered and bit into her burger. After our second round of lovemaking, I couldn't go any longer without real food. I made a quick trip out to grab us the biggest, greasiest burgers I could find and a ridiculously large order of French fries to share.

"Can we spend the day together tomorrow?" I blurted. I had been trying not to smother her with questions in the last few hours since she'd arrived at my door. I'd missed her desperately and having her in my midst for only a little while, a clean slate ahead of us, sent my mind speeding toward our future. I wanted it all, but I'd settle for a Tuesday.

She gave me a side-eyed grin, finishing the fries she'd just put in her mouth. "No."

My brow furrowed.

"I have a job interview tomorrow."

"Sloane, that's great! Where?"

"The Salem Historical Society. It's an assistant marketing manager position. It's at eleven so we can meet up after."

"That's so great. I'm happy for you. I...I'm sorry I haven't been as supportive about your work. I—"

I shook my head when Sloane's hand landed on mine softly. Before either of us could say anything else, I heard my phone ringing in the bedroom and hopped up to get it. When I reached the nightstand, my chest ached as I viewed the name on the screen. My eyes darted to the door, thinking of Sloane sitting in the kitchen finishing her food as I held my breath before answering.

"Hello?"

"Hey," Marie said on the other end.

I hadn't spoken to my sister since Oliver's wedding. Dad told me she'd gone to the hospital with Warren but that was the last thing I'd heard. Just like with Sloane, I was too ashamed to reach out to her. I was also still angry with her for having him there in the first place.

"Hi, Marie. Is everything all right?"

I always asked. No matter what drama was going down between the two of us, I cared about her and I would never stop being there for Barry if he needed me.

"Are you busy?"

A lump formed in my throat. "No. I'm at home. What's going on?"

She sighed. "Nothing. But I'm in town and I was hoping I could come by. So we can talk."

I exhaled through my nose and clamped my lips together tightly for a moment. "Sloane's here. You're welcome to come by but I won't ask her to leave."

"Barry is with me so maybe he could sit with her while we talk?"

The familiar flare of anger I often felt when my sister got an inch but took a mile lit through my sternum and I grumbled. "Marie, that's a bit presumptuous. If you need to talk to me just come over. We'll sort it out when you get here."

I heard her retreat at the sound of my angry voice and a little squeak came from the back of her throat. I let out a breath, trying like hell to remember even one word from my anger support group.

"We're outside," she said.

Shit. I gritted my teeth and nodded. "Just give me a minute. I'll be right there."

I hung up and grabbed a shirt, yanking it over my head as I headed into the kitchen where Sloane was rinsing her plate. She heard me approach and turned around. "Everything okay?"

We'd agreed, nothing between us holding us back. No running away from the hard stuff. I just hated to bring Marie and Barry and all that they reminded us of into our perfect night of reconciliation.

"Marie is here. She wants to talk to me. I'm so sorry. I know it's awkward but—"

"She's family, Leo."

The look on Sloane's face didn't hold a hint of annoyance and in fact, her eyes warmed with compassion. Just as I heard the knock at the door, I pulled her close and kissed her hair, breathing in her scent and letting her arms around my waist ease my worry for a second. As I went to let them in she ducked into my bedroom to put on something less revealing and was out again by the time Barry barreled into the living room.

"Uncle Leo, can I watch TV?"

"Can you say 'hello' first?" I chided.

He gave me a grin then pointed to the television once more. I sighed but when he noticed Sloane, his smile grew.

"Miss Sloane!"

"Hey, buddy. Do you want to help me with something in the backyard?"

His eyes lit up and he looked to his mother. Marie was standing in the entryway, one step behind me, wringing her hands.

She smiled and nodded her permission. "Thank you, Sloane," Marie said.

I glanced at my sister then back to Sloane.

"Sure thing," Sloane replied as she took Barry by the hand and walked him outside through the sliding glass door.

In the silence of my home, I turned to Marie and gestured toward the living room. She followed me to the couch. I didn't sense anger in her, so I figured she hadn't come to fight, but I still worried about what the conversation would hold. She let out a deep sigh and turned to me finally ready to speak.

"I just wanted to tell you that Warren and I are finished. For good this time."

Before I could stifle it, an incredulous noise barked from my lungs and my eyes bounced to the ceiling.

"I mean it," Marie said firmly. "He crossed a line. It's done."

My gaze snapped to my sister and immediately scanned her for bruises. I'm sure she saw the look in my eyes as I searched her face, her neck and wrists. Relief washed over my mind as she shook her head under my scrutinizing stare.

"No, not that. But he said awful things. Things he can't take back. Things about you. Sloane..." Her voice trailed off and her eyes welled with tears. "And Barry."

The voices of my ever-calm group therapy leaders lilted in my ear. *Think before you speak. Take a beat.* I let the hateful words I had for Warren disintegrate on my tongue and opted to support my sister with my words instead.

"I'm sorry, Marie."

She looked at me and nodded. "Me too."

"I'm sorry I hit him. Not because he didn't deserve it— he deserved worse—"

Marie laughed lightly. "He got worse."

My brow furrowed as I waited for her to explain. A sinister smirk made its way to her mouth—a look I'd never seen my sister wear.

"I told his wife. Everything."

"Shit," I whispered before a chuckle rolled through me.

"Yeah. So I think the money is going to dry up since he's going to be dealing with a divorce," she said. "Mom and Dad think I should sue him for child support. I haven't decided yet. I'm just going to keep working and try to do it on my own for a while."

I wanted to tell her I was proud of her, but I hated to sound patronizing. She didn't need my praise. She fidgeted on the couch beside me, maybe with more to say.

"Anyway, I just wanted to tell you I'm really sorry. You were always right about him and I never listened. I need to apologize to Sloane, too."

I nodded. As badly as I didn't want to shame my sister

now that she'd concluded on her own that her ex was a world class asshole, I wanted better for Sloane. She'd been a victim of Warren's deceit in the same way Marie had; she'd never deserved the dirty looks and the cold shoulder.

We talked a little more before Marie headed out back. I watched from my living room window while Barry picked rocks out of my flower beds and Marie and Sloane stood face to face in the yard. Marie's arms were folded over her chest as she spoke, averting her eyes to the grass. Sloane's soft features morphed into a tender smile and after a few minutes her arms stretched out hesitantly.

My sister wiped tears from her eyes and slowly opened herself up for the offered embrace. Marie and Sloane hugged each other tightly and my chest constricted. The healing I saw between them, even without knowing the words they'd shared, relieved an ache that had sat within me since the night Sloane found out Barry was Warren's son. The last hurdle had been cleared. My family was Sloane's family. Nothing was left between us, holding us back. Nothing remained but the future.

CHAPTER TWENTY-ONE

FOUR MONTHS LATER

Sloane

I sipped my water, ignoring the scrutinizing looks from Bryon, Craig, and my sister, Ellie. They didn't dare ask the reason for me not partaking in the bottle of champagne Bryon had brought for the celebration. Funny that they didn't seem to notice or care that Leo hadn't had a drop of alcohol either. I glanced at Leo after checking the clock and felt a surge of excitement. It was almost time.

"Time for gifts?" Craig asked.

I smiled and nodded. Bryon happily handed a gift bag to Elizabeth and whispered in her ear. She toddled toward me with it, tugging at the pink tissue paper poking out.

"Happy happy!" she cooed proudly as she handed me the bag. Everyone laughed at the sound of her sweet voice and the new words she'd learned.

"That's right, Lizzy!" Craig cheered. "Happy Birthday, Aunt Sloane."

"Happy happy," she said again as I let her pull the tempting tissue paper out of the bag for me.

"Thank you, sweet girl."

I reached in the bag and pulled out a large pale pink coffee mug with gold cursive letters that said, "Best Aunt Ever." I reached to squeeze Elizabeth to my side and she squirmed away with a giggle. Standing to hug and kiss Bryon's cheek, I thanked him and Craig.

My sister looked sheepish and handed me a card next. "I'm sorry I suck," Ellie said.

"Stop it," I chided her. Inside the card was a gift certificate to the salon where I got my hair done. I assured her it was perfect and thanked her.

Leo let a hand find the hair at the back of my neck. "I was wondering if you were starting to grow it out," he mused.

I eyed him and remembered his first reaction to my shorter haircut. "Just a little overdue," I replied with a grin.

He matched my look, the sexual tension simmering between us. Leo reached behind him and handed me a package, much to my surprise. He'd already told me a few days ago that my gift would be waiting for me later. We were heading for dinner at Melanie and Gabe's house in a little while and after that, our reason for not drinking —playtime.

I eyed him coyly. "What's this?"

He glanced down at the package in my hands and nodded for me to open it. I had a clue what the thick rectangular object might be, but I bit my bottom lip when I tore the wrapping paper to reveal a leather-bound copy of *The Scarlett Letter*.

"Open it," he said. I heard it as a command rather than a suggestion and my stomach quivered.

The firm cover opened. I expected to see something hidden inside but it was just the book. My eyes narrowed on Leo, but his expression urged me on and I begrudgingly began to skim the pages. That's when I noticed. Just past the beginning of the second chapter was the first of many wrinkled and stained pages. This wasn't just any leather-bound copy. It was ours. It was the reason we met the way we did and the reason for my very first punishment. I blushed and closed the book gently.

"Thank you," I whispered.

"You're welcome, my love," he replied, a grin twitching at his lips.

"You like that book?" Ellie asked.

I'd almost forgotten we were surrounded by other people and that all eyes were on me. I stuck on a smile and nodded casually. "I love the classics."

She made a noise then gasped. "Oh! Speaking of infidelity! Did you hear about your old boss?"

I coughed and shot quick looks at the boys. "What? No."

"His wife found out he'd been cheating. *For years.* Turns out he was even embezzling money from the firm to pay these women off!" Ellie exclaimed. "The firm closed, he's filing bankruptcy, she's going to bleed him dry in the divorce, and he might even face criminal charges. It's big drama."

Of course, I'd already heard it from Bryon and Leo had heard it from Marie. Warren's life was the proverbial dumpster fire and there was no doubt he deserved it. But those of us he'd left in his wake through the years hadn't. The people at the firm who lost their jobs, his daughter, and Barry hadn't asked to be a part of his mess, yet they would suffer the consequences of his horrible decisions.

I muttered something about it being terrible and shocking while Leo squeezed my hand. Warren would always be there in the background somewhere. We couldn't erase him entirely and honestly, I didn't see a point in trying. He was no longer important to my story—written out of the novel entirely, in fact. I smiled thinking of the way Leo had brought up the subject of my novel a few months ago. He wouldn't let it drop. I'd found pristinely perfect notebooks and pens that wrote so smoothly they'd make a teacher swoon waiting for me on the kitchen table one night. He would charge my laptop and make me a cup of tea, encouraging me to take a look at my work instead of turning on an episode of whatever we were binging. At first, I assured him I no longer needed to write. It had been my way of working through the initial pain I'd felt when I arrived in Salem and that had passed. But the man could read me so well. He saw the words brimming in me when I didn't.

So I started over.

I deleted the Warren character without a thought and

eventually scrapped the whole thing. It was slow going but I was happy to be working on a project for myself again. Of course, the fact that I'd come to the bookstore on my days off and set up shop in my old writing space—the second floor—surely pleased Leo. He tried not to bother me while I was working but you know what they say about all work and no play....

"We should head out," Craig said, glancing at his watch.

My cheeks felt flushed as I snapped out of my head in time to hug my family and friends goodbye. We exchanged love and goodbyes and soon it was just me and Leo in my apartment.

Our eyes locked. His hand rose to his mouth and his whole demeanor changed as he dragged his thumbnail over his bottom lip. I swallowed thickly then let the anticipatory feelings consume me.

The heady lust in his gaze made me smile wickedly. I nearly moaned when he wet his lips.

"You ready for your party?" he asked with a grin.

I nodded.

"You have no idea what you're in for, my love."

His eyes blazed like butane fire and my stomach dropped as he grabbed his car keys and snapped his fingers.

———

Dessert was gone. The laughter waned and though I'd only been to one party, I recognized the lull in conversation that signaled the games were about to begin. Leo's hand slipped onto my knee, squeezing it firmly. Jade slinked out from under the table where she'd already begun purring and headed down the hall with Ben following closely. Gabe and Melanie made eyes at each other while the other two couples, people I'd only met this evening, stood and disappeared into the various rooms.

Part of me wanted to relive that first party and have a look at what everyone else was doing before we embarked on whatever Leo had planned. But tonight was my party, one I had no doubt would surpass that first experience.

"Everything is set up just like you asked," Melanie said to Leo with a seductive grin.

He ran his tongue along his teeth behind closed lips. My stomach twisted delightfully watching his mannerisms change and take on that of my Sir.

Melanie turned to me with the same look of lust and power, gazing upon me as though I were a second round of dessert. "Happy Birthday, Sloane," she said. "Enjoy."

I gulped and looked to Leo. He softened for the time being and offered his hand to me as we stood up. I boldly clutched his arm as we walked hand in hand down the hall in silence. It didn't begin until he said so and I took full advantage of my last few minutes of freedom. Leo leaned in to me and kissed my hair as we approached a closed door. He stopped in front of it and turned to me, clasping my hands and looking meaningfully into my eyes.

"Do you know your colors, lovely girl?"

I grinned and nodded.

"Do you know how much I love you?"

I drew in a deep breath and let my eyes close for a moment as I smiled. "Yes," I sighed. "And I love you."

He smiled the way I'd come to love—the gentle smile that was more in his eyes than on his mouth. And just like that, he dropped my hands and reached into his jacket, pulling out a pair of black leather gloves. I trained my eyes to the floor and breathed another deep breath, readying myself as best I could for what waited for me. He'd told me a few days ago that he had something big planned and that I should prepare for the unexpected.

Leo opened the door and walked in first, then smoothly commanded, "Come."

My feet led me to the center of the room but I didn't look around, waiting to be ordered. I felt him come up behind me, drawing the zipper of my dress down and slipping the fabric off my shoulders, casting it to the floor. He'd asked me not to wear a bra or panties when I'd gotten dressed for dinner, and he left me standing completely bare for him, now in only my heels.

My curiosity piqued when I noticed how warm the room felt despite my nudity. My eyes quickly bounced up to survey my surroundings. There was a space heater in the corner and white candles lit on every surface. I saw a long table covered in every tool of pleasure and pain imaginable. A chair sat off to one side and I recognized it as the same one I'd pushed Leo into back when I'd worn the leather gloves. Finally my eyes noticed the structure I stood underneath.

Dark espresso wood beams made a four-posted frame

with two beams across the top that reminded me of the outdoor pergola I'd been hinting for Leo to build for his deck. A thick steel hook anchored into the center of the crossbeams overhead and from that hung a metal triangle. My brows knit together as I attempted to make sense of the structure and its purpose.

While my mind connected dots, trying to anticipate Leo's plan, the soft tickle of a feather trailed up my spine and I shivered.

"Oh, no shivering, my love. That one was free. Any more will cost you," Leo said.

I inhaled sharply through my nose and firmed my feet underneath me. I remembered this game. I played it well. He moved in front of me and used two fingers to lift my chin so our eyes met. He dusted the feather over my breasts, the soft tease pebbling my nipples instantly. A little smirk twitched on his face and he stepped to the table of devices, setting the feather down in line. As Leo ran his gloved hand along his many options, I let my eyes drift up to the wood constructed around us again.

A quick snap against my ass made me shut my eyes.

"You'll find out what it is soon enough," Leo said, reading the curiosity in me. Another snap on the opposite cheek and I knew it was a riding crop. When he walked around to face me again, he dragged the inch and a half of folded leather at the end of a whip stick across my jaw and down my body. He gave me another quick snap on the calf and I jumped, pulling my foot up at the unexpected sting.

"That's one."

I bit my lip, trying not to smile. Yes, I was good at playing this game, but I also liked the consequences.

Next came our old favorite, the Wartenberg wheel. Leo began to hum quietly as he rolled the tines over my skin, creating and tracing goosebumps at the same time. I shut my eyes to feel the prickles better and focused on the sound of Leo's humming as he toyed with me. Suddenly, I recognized the tune and my eyes flashed open. He grinned at me and kept humming "Almost Paradise" as he rolled the spiked wheel down to my thin line of pubic hair. I gasped and jumped when he slipped the metal wheel into the crease between my legs, the tines prickling against my wet clit.

"Two," he said smoothly, resuming the song instantly.

I sighed and watched him move toward the table once more. My gut trembled thinking of what he might choose next. When I saw him pull a long white candle from its holder, I moaned. Leo glanced over his shoulder at me, brows cinched together, and wickedly placed the candle back in the brass stand. He faced me and unfastened his jacket, laying it on the chair. His fingers worked the buttons of his crisp white shirt and he tossed it over his jacket. I sucked my bottom lip into my mouth, feeling saliva flow at the sight of his half naked body. The lean cut of his abs and the thick veins in his neck tempted me to reach out for him but I didn't dare.

He turned to the tools and I stared at the lion painted over the muscles of his back and shoulders. I wanted to run my tongue along the tattoo, tasting the warmth of his skin. When he turned to face me, I felt a little disappointment noticing he didn't have anything in his hand for me. Then I saw silver flash as he opened and closed one gloved fist. He raised one hand to me and waved fingers tipped with what looked like talons—silver nails that he'd capped over his fingertips that stopped at his knuckles.

His eyes darkened. The lion was ready to dig his claws into me.

Leo approached and smoothed the simple black glove over one side of my rounded bottom. Then the clawed glove stroked the other side, scraping the tender flesh enough to make me cry out. Leo covered my mouth with his in a passionate kiss that sent a shudder rolling through me from tongue to tailbone.

"Three," he said then nipped at my top lip. "And four."

I huffed a breath but held my next as he dragged all five claws down my arm. I looked down to see white lines turn red. The attachments were sharp enough to redden and mark but not enough to break the skin. He pulled one sharp fingertip across my collarbone, his tongue following behind it, licking the newly marred skin devilishly.

"Breathe," he whispered before capturing one of my nipples in his mouth.

I sighed and my chest heaved. Leo's palm cupped my breast as he continued to suck my nipple roughly. I screamed when he squeezed his hand, letting the talons dig into my supple flesh. He straightened and tapped my open lips with keen fingertips.

"Five."

My knees had begun to quake beneath me. The swift

changing of his methods had me nearing the edge of the dark pool I loved diving into. I felt every touch, tender or torturous, on a heightened level. Every breath made the stings and scratches hum a little louder on my skin. And as close to spinning out as I felt, I knew we were nowhere close to finished.

Leo dropped to his knees and I mustered all my willpower not to thread my hands through his hair and pull his mouth toward my body. I looked down at him and he stared up at me. With one silver claw, he scratched the soft place where my abdomen ended and my sex began. Four quick scratches and he smiled. Then another single scratch followed by three more. He ended with a series of four and I felt the area stinging, welts rising where he'd scratched deeper than he had anywhere else on my body. Leo sat back on his heels and stared at his work and I had to know what he was grinning about. I looked down and saw a word he'd once drawn in me in almost the same spot.

Mine.

Now written on my skin more like a brand than a lipstick tattoo, I felt it deeper than I did all those months ago. I was his. Leo licked his lips and stared at the word then flicked his gaze to me again. His tongue darted out and licked the freshly marked flesh, soothing it for a moment.

Leo rose and I felt myself wobble a little. Standing in heels while he'd played with me in new and old ways alike had weakened me. He put a gentle hand on my shoulder, the glove without claws, and steadied me.

"How would you like to get off your feet?" he asked.

"Yes, please, Sir," I whispered.

A wicked laugh came from the back of his throat and he popped off each of the five finger claws and placed them with the other instruments. The clang of metal sent electricity through my veins. I watched as Leo anchored two chains to the steel triangle that hung from the wooden beams. Dangling from the chains were two thin black straps and three thick belt-like leather straps. When he motioned for me to come to him my feet stuttered forward. He moved me so my back was to the hanging leather and steel.

"Hold on like this," he said, moving my hands to grip the chain on either side.

"Now lean back and sit down," he said.

My stomach pitched but I did as he told, letting myself lean backwards. One thick leather belt caught me like a swing or a saddle, a thick hammock across my lower back, the two other straps split to cradle my ass. I rocked on my heels a little then let the swing completely hold my bodyweight.

I glanced up at him and smiled before boldly pushing off the ground and pumping my legs to swing like a child. Though Leo smiled too, he reached out to grab the chains, stopping the motion. In a few quick movements, he hoisted my legs up one at a time and secured the remaining leather straps under my thighs, anchoring them in place. I sat locked in place, slightly tilted back, legs spread for him, my body at his mercy.

Suspended in air, I knew what this was.

This was my gift.

Leo cleared his throat and smoothed his leather gloves from my knees down my thighs, then spread me apart. I was at the perfect level for him to fuck me. But I knew I had to get my punishment first.

"I thought about the flogger. Or maybe a paddle. But I know how much you like a good old-fashioned spanking and since it's your birthday..."

I wriggled against him and the rig, not sure of what I hoped to achieve in doing so. Every draft of air against my pussy made me feel wetter and now that I was anticipating all the swing had to offer, I ached for release.

"Squirmy girl. Should I double that five to ten?"

My breath caught. *Yes.*

"I'll count, my love. You just remember to breathe."

With the first crack of his hand against my ass, I curled inward and the chains rattled. My head whipped up and saw a quick glimpse of Leo's hand as it reared back again. It was bare. He'd removed a glove to spank me harder. When his palm came down on me for a second time I grunted but didn't thrash. His skin against mine stung worse than the leather gloves I adored. By the time he got to six, I felt the familiar fog roll in and I shut my eyes. Relaxing further into the swing, I let my head fall back and took the last few spanks.

"That's it," Leo rasped.

My eyes blinked open and he stood above my head looking down at me lovingly. He leaned in and held my face, kissing my temple.

"Thank you, lovely girl. Thank you for everything," he whispered.

Blanketed by the drowsiness of pleasure and pain, I closed my eyes again just as silk slipped over my eyes. Leo tied the fabric at the back of my head and wasted no time letting his hands smooth down my torso, toying with my breasts.

I huffed a breath as he pinched and rolled my nipples. His touch walked a border between a caress and something cruel. With my sight stolen and no firm connection to the ground, I was more at his mercy than I'd ever been. Every rough touch he offered made me swing and in turn made my stomach quiver. I moaned when his tongue slipped into the intricate petals of my sex.

Leo devoured me, unrelentingly fucking me with his tongue and sucking my clit so deeply I ground my teeth and screamed as an orgasm shattered me. My whimpering breaths broke the air. I tried to come down but he wouldn't stop. He pushed thick leather fingers inside me. First one in my pussy, then a second and soon one digit entered my ass and I shook again, crying out as another crashing wave of ecstasy bombarded me.

Three fingers sunk as deep in me as possible then stroked along my inner walls, saying "come hither," beckoning my pleasure to come out and play. Another finger twirled a lazy circle inside my ass and his mouth continued to envelope my clit, lapping at my arousal like a starving cat too hungry to ever give up this never-ending meal.

I stopped breathing and Leo felt it. His fingers worked

faster and faster, clawing his leather padded fingertips against the honeyed core that ached for him. As a third detonation melted through me like lava, tears streamed from the corners of my eyes and my arms fell back, no longer able to grip the chains of my seat. I heard the clanging of metal, my chains rattling as my body shook uncontrollably.

His hands slipped out of my body, the emptiness turning my silent tears to a full-on sob. "Breathe," he commanded, letting his hands settle on my hips. "Take a breath, my love." My lungs obeyed barely, sipping in the slightest amount of oxygen.

And then I was full again.

The smooth length of his shaft had moved inside my body to the hilt. My hands extended toward him, but I couldn't reach. I couldn't see him. But I could feel him. I continued to struggle to reach him, whimpering and flexing my fingers. As his cock slid out of me, dragging along every sparking and sputtering nerve in my pussy, his fingers laced with mine. I sighed relief, my head falling back once more as his warm bare fingers squeezed mine tightly.

Leo used our locked hands to push and pull me, fucking me in a rhythm so spellbinding my hands went limp and soon he was holding me by the wrists. I sank into the dizzying, dark place in my mind as Leo sank into my body over and over again. His breathing grew erratic, grunting with each thrust, though it sounded miles away. He dropped my wrists in favor of gripping my thighs and my arms flopped at my sides. With barely any energy left, I concentrated on the sound of each of his panting breaths on the air and the feeling of another orgasm building within me.

Leo growled, slamming into me harder. The sounds of metal clanging and sweat slipping on leather straps and bodies fusing together echoed in my fogged mind.

"I love you," he choked out, gripping the flesh of my thighs.

The throb between my legs intensified and the warmth of Leo coming inside me pushed me over the edge one more time. I cried out and my body clenched around Leo's cock, simultaneously begging him to stay and forcing him out with every muscular pulse. Pleasure rolled through me in waves and the dark haze enveloped me more, pulling me deeper into the depths of my perfect agony. The lovely duality was something only Leo could bestow upon me. The place where pain and pleasure met—where control ceased on my part and chaos reigned. My Sir, my demon, my lionhearted love ruled me so profoundly I was able to let go and enjoy the levitating spin my mind offered.

When he pulled himself from my core, my body shook and my breath heaved. And when I thought it was over, Leo doled out one final spank—cracking his palm hard against my ass. I cried out and my pussy constricted again, and I heard his voice drift into my head like a distant song.

"And one to grow on," he said with a laugh. "Happy Birthday, lovely girl."

With that, Leo gripped the back of my knee and flung me to one side, propelling the swing. Air whooshed over my naked body. Centrifugal force pinned me with my arms and head rested back. I was no longer spinning out in my mind only.

My body trembled—pussy pulsing, toes curling, teeth chattering, flesh buzzing.

I succumbed to the spin just like I always did. I didn't wonder when it would stop or if Leo would do the stopping. Instead I chose to let go. Bound by leather, bound by devotion, bound by trust, and bound by love, I let the scene and both the mental and physical spin consume me.

My breath came easier and my heartbeat settled but I continued to twirl, suspended in air. My skin no longer tingled from his touch and my insides no longer tightened in his absence, but I still reveled in the pirouette with which he'd gifted me.

The fog lifted from my mind and light crept in to push out the darkness as he removed my blindfold...but I kept spinning. I'd always be spinning. Because Leo Calloway had turned my life into gorgeous carousel.

As the swing slowed, my senses returned. I pulled myself upright, gripping the chains. I blinked and found myself staring into Leo's eyes. He took my face in his hands and we spoke in unison the same words—the only words we had after everything that had happened to bring us to this exquisite moment.

"Thank you."

EPILOGUE

Leo

I kissed her softly and thanked her again. She slowly opened her eyes and I helped her get steady on her feet. I found the clothes she'd been wearing and covered her, leading her to a sofa on the other end of the room.

Sloane sat, clutching the soft cotton dress to her body, and sighed before smiling. She looked around the space and her eyes narrowed. "Have we ever played in this room before?"

I laughed and glanced around, nodding. "You know, I think it's our first time in here. Finally, after twelve years of dinner parties at Gabe and Melanie's, we've christened every room."

Sloane's brow rose and she shot me a sultry look. "What an accomplishment," she said, leaning in to kiss me.

With gentle fingers I pulled at the fabric she used like a

blanket and took a look at the redness on her right breast. "Are you all right?"

She looked down at the red line above her nipple and shrugged. "It doesn't hurt anymore."

We'd only used the violet wand a handful of times, but Sloane's alabaster skin clearly was more sensitive to it than I'd realized. She slipped the dress over her head and stood up, letting it fall over her body. I followed her lead and found my clothes strewn about the room, dressing myself as I picked up each piece. We both stepped into our shoes then our eyes caught and we laughed.

"Good night?" I asked.

"Yes, Sir," Sloane replied. Her hand met mine and I felt the familiar burst of joy I felt every time I saw the sparkling diamond on her left ring finger.

As we headed down the hall toward Gabe and Melanie's front door, we saw another door open and a couple emerge. They both had flushed faces and damp hair-lines. When they saw us they grinned sheepishly.

"You guys leaving too?" Mira asked.

"Yeah, we only have our babysitter until eleven," Sloane answered.

Mira smiled and embraced Sloane sweetly. I extended my hand to her husband, a man I never dreamed I'd call a friend.

"Good to see you, Ethan," I said.

"Goodnight, guys," Ethan replied, shaking my hand and giving Sloane a side-hug.

In the car, Sloane leaned her seat back and sighed,

letting her eyes drift closed for a moment. My fingers inched toward her knee and crept up her thigh, listening as she hummed her approval. After all this time she was still insatiable.

The drive back to our house this time of night was too quick, another round would have to wait. We walked inside through the garage and the smell of pizza permeated the downstairs. The blue glow of the television lit the living room and the face of our babysitter as he stood to greet us.

"Hey guys, how was your date?"

Sloane kept her smile innocent enough and simply told him it was nice.

"Were the kids okay for you?" I asked.

He laughed and shook his head. "They were fine. A little rowdy but we had a good time like always. Dominic will probably have a bruise on his cheek tomorrow from a run in with the coffee table. And Quinn wanted me to show you the picture she colored for you; it's on the refrigerator."

Sloane and I both glanced back at the bright coloring page on the fridge and smiled.

"So what's the going rate these days?" I asked, opening my wallet.

"Oh...just enough for gas I guess."

I met his deep brown eyes meaningfully and felt my chest tighten with sentiment. He'd grown into such a wonderful young man.

"Barry, you stop that. We appreciate you coming over so much. Just because you're family doesn't mean you work for free," Sloane said, slipping between us and handing over two fifties from my billfold. She pinned me with a speedy, nearly unnoticeable glare, keeping me from balking at the monetary exchange.

Barry dragged a hand through his brunette curls and looked at me hesitantly, the money still in his hand.

I softened and nodded at him. "Just drive home safe okay? Text us when you get there?"

He beamed and for a split second he was still four years old. Sloane hugged him first and then I pulled him close. No matter how tall he got—an inch from passing me up—he was still that precocious child we both adored. I patted him on the back and walked him to the door, reminding him one more time to check in when he arrived home. Sloane stood at my side as we watched Barry pull out of the driveway, and when his taillights diminished into the night my hand drifted to her ass, grabbing a handful.

"A hundred dollars?" I whispered.

She chuckled and looked up at me impishly, batting her eyelashes and pressing her ruby lips together.

"Bratty wife," I growled against her ear. "What am I going to do with you?"

She turned into my body, slid her hands delicately up my chest, and whispered, "Take me upstairs, Sir."

ACKNOWLEDGMENTS

Thank you to every person who waited patiently for this conclusion. A tiny human came into my world and put a lot of things on hold for longer than I expected (including this book) but so many of you understood and supported my slow and steady pace while I sorted out my first year of motherhood. Thank you for waiting. Thank you for still reading this book. Thank you for wanting to see Leo and Sloane's HEA just as badly as I wanted to write it.

To Britni Hill, I love you sister. I don't know if I'd be on number ten were it not for you, your friendship, and your support.

Thank you to Mo, a fabulous blogger, friend, and an amazing beta reader.

To JBZ, my very own Bryon, I adore you. Thanks for being my hype man.

Thank you to my incredible editor Erin and to my proofreader at All Good Things Editing.

Thank you to Ben Murray for your photograph and to Jordon Blackwell and Kaitlyn Gibson for unknowingly bringing two characters to life for me.

And lastly, thank you to my son for not only being the brightest light in my life, but also for finally learning how to take a nap so Mommy could finish this damn book. Love you.

ABOUT THE AUTHOR

Published since 2012, Kate Roth is addicted to all things romance. Her passion for love stories, both traditional and unconventional, has led her to write in various sub-genres of romance. She is inspired by everything from music to the real-life romance tales she's heard through her years as a professional hair stylist.

Kate spends her time away from the keyboard with her insta-love husband, her sweet baby boy and faithful pound puppy.

ALSO BY KATE ROTH

The Low Notes

Reckless Radiance

The Confession Records Collection

Natural Harmony

Sway

The Desire Resort Series

Last Resort

Best Laid Plans

Peachy Keen

The Bindings Duet

Bindings

Leather Bound